G R JORDAN

The Express Wishes of Mr MacIver

A Kirsten Stewart Thriller

'A diamond is a chunk of coal that did
really well under pressure'

Henry Kissinger

Contents

Foreword

This story is set in the areas of Inverness, Tain and the north of Scotland. Although incorporating known cities, towns and villages, note that all events, persons, vessels and specific places are fictional and not to be confused with actual buildings and structures which have been used as an inspirational canvas to tell a completely fictional story.

Acknowledgement

To Susan, Jean and Rosemary for your work in bringing this novel to completion, your time and effort is deeply appreciated.

Novels by G R Jordan

Chapter 1

Kirsten Stewart looked down upon the gathering, knowing that they were unaware of her bird's-eye view. The rafters of the barn were undisturbed by the small lights below that showed a gathering of approximately eight people. A number of them had guns, not yet drawn, but Kirsten had seen the shape of them inside tight jackets or caught the occasional glimpse when a longer garment had opened. It had been five hours since she had climbed up into the barn's roof. She was thankful she didn't suffer from vertigo, because the perch she wanted had required her to manoeuvre into a precarious position, a spot where the directional mic could pick up the conversation below for her team outside.

'It's loud and clear,' said a voice in her earpiece.

She tapped the earpiece twice, not wanting to say anything herself, lest it be picked up by any of the gathering below.

'Delta in position.' The hoarse Scottish voice brought Kirsten some comfort, knowing that her team were outside. Dominic was not on his own, but had the police firearms team with him, ready to sweep in when ready. The firearm officers were well trained and had handled operations of a similar nature before by themselves, but the go signal would come from Kirsten.

Only when she had gathered enough information.

She thought about the fifty-year-old man she had recently employed, an intelligence specialist. He'd initially worked within the UK before moving overseas. An operation had gone bad in one of the Middle Eastern states, and Kirsten knew that he was receiving treatment for it on a weekly basis. When she'd interviewed him, he was as sharp as anything. All the tests she gave him, like all of his candid answers, satisfied her. Dominic was the solid centre she wanted on her team.

In her late twenties, Kirsten was young to have risen to the position she was in, running the North of Scotland intelligence. Her boss, Anna Hunt, had seen fit to lift her up. Although it may have been due to an incident which brought to light a number of officers who were not loyal, and had their fingers in other pies outside of the service, Anna Hunt had given no indication the promotion was neither undeserved nor unwise.

'Charlie in position.'

Charlie was Carrie-Anne, a woman who was also older than Kirsten, although she'd barely reached forty. She had a strong Welsh accent and had come recommended by Anna Hunt. When Kirsten had asked Justin Chivers, the communications expert, if he'd heard of Carrie-Anne, the man had nodded and smiled, in the way that he did whenever he talked about any woman. Beyond the amorous ideas, he'd also explained how good an analyst the woman was, able to see within the information much that others could not. While primarily being an analyst, she was also capable of helping out on operations, so Carrie-Anne was a natural addition to the team.

Kirsten leaned forward, trying to get a better view of the faces below. On the trail today was diamonds. A noise had been heard that diamonds were on the move, and not just ordinary ones, but one specific one. Although the team was unsure of what it actually was, the amount of chatter and noise around criminal networks had made it something of interest and Kirsten was keen to find out more about it. In many ways, she had a roving brief and the fact that outside agencies were involved—foreign countries were after the gem—made it part of Kirsten's portfolio. She coordinated, of course, with the police, and that's why they were here as well, but her team was running this operation, so she needed to get it right.

Currently, she'd been up in the rafters for over five hours, but the meeting below had only been going on for ten minutes. There were two sides who clearly did not trust the other, but both were waiting for another person to arrive. It looked like there might be an auction of some sort, although Kirsten was unsure. The seller was from the continent, that much Kirsten knew, but beyond that, everything was rumour and conjecture. It was only due to Justin's work tapping the phones of local criminals that she'd been able to pick up the noise about the diamond and eventually trace it through communications to this barn.

Kirsten thought back to earlier that afternoon when she'd been in a hotel lying back in a Jacuzzi, allowing it to soak into her muscles. She had made sure she had taken a little time in the afternoon, as she was going to be out most of the night. Besides, she didn't have to answer to anyone anymore. Well, maybe Anna Hunt, who was her direct boss and overall in charge of Scottish operations. Anna was rarely in Inverness, with Kirsten often having to travel down to Glasgow or Edinburgh to meet her.

'Where the hell is he? He said he'd be here.'

'Calm your trunks. No need to get uppity yet. The man said

he'll be here.'

'Well, I don't like it. I don't like sitting here with you lot. You don't do auctions like this.'

'Don't do auctions like what? You got a problem with me, mister?'

Kirsten watched two of the men down below step up and come close, their faces locked together tight, staring each other out.

'Now, now,' said a third man. 'That won't get us anywhere. If he sees anything wrong or any trouble in here, he's going to run, isn't he? Neither of you are going to end up with that diamond, so enough.'

Kirsten breathed a sigh of relief, because the last thing she needed was a gunfight before the goods arrived. Kirsten tapped her microphone three times.

'Delta here. No, not been seen. Target not acquired.'

Kirsten was getting fed up. It was usual for sellers to arrive on time; otherwise, how could clients trust them? This one was running late. Maybe they'd gone bust, or maybe something was wrong. Kirsten tapped for her other colleague on the microphone.

'Charlie here, we'll check.' She had instructed Carrie-Anne to make a sweep of the area, to see if anyone was approaching the barn, while Dominic stood with the police firearms team, ready to enter the barn at a moment's notice. Carrie-Anne was on her own, moving in and out of the shadows, acting as Kirsten's other arm, keeping the area safe and watching for any intruders.

'Nothing found. Charlie out.'

Kirsten moved back in the rafters, carefully looking around at her escape route down. The far side of the barn had hay she could drop into, but she'd have to move quickly. On her head were infrared goggles, and Dominic had already identified the power source that led to the lights in the barn. Although they were dim, they were certainly providing enough light so that the current occupants could see each other. Thankfully, however, the light wasn't so strong and Kirsten reckoned she could drop down to the hay without being seen as long as she didn't make a noise in the fall.

'This is a bust. Where is he? He knows we're sitting here with all this cash.'

One of the men down below spun and looked at the man who had made the comment. He was clearly annoyed with him.

'We don't talk money on the job, do we?' With that he stepped across and slapped the man with the back of his hand across the face. It clearly hurt. The man became subservient quickly. 'And it comes with firepower behind it, so understand that, okay? It's well protected.' The man moved his jacket back. Kirsten could identify the gun on the man's hip.

'But there's five of us,' said the man. 'Only three of you. I doubt you'll be standing.'

'I'll be standing. You won't stand, you clown. I'll bury you deep.'

'Let's just take a wee chill here. Come on,' said an older voice. 'We're here for a reason. It's not gunfight at the O.K. Corral.'

'I don't like how he's looking now. Look at him. Look at the way he's looking at me.'

The original speaker stepped forward to the one who had challenged him about the money and spat in his face. Kirsten saw the punch being thrown, but more than that, she saw the men behind starting to reach for weapons.

'Execute, execute, execute,' said Kirsten. 'All hot. All hot.'

Kirsten knew her team would be on the move, but nimbly she ran along the rafters, dropping down into the hay while pulling on her night vision goggles. As she came off the rafter, all the lights went out.

When she hit the hay, she scrambled out over the top of it and noted the guns in the room. She stepped behind one man, incapacitating him with a kick into the back of his knees and a full-blooded punch to the back of the head. The door burst open. Several police officers, also with night vision goggles on and rifles in front of them, stepped forward. Kirsten saw a man on her right who was pulling a gun out from his jacket suddenly freeze as he heard the words, 'Police, police. You're covered. Weapons down. Weapons down.'

Kirsten scanned either side of her quickly and saw one man continue to react with his weapon. She launched a kick to his hand and the weapon fell from it. She drove him to the ground with her other arm, pinning him. He probably had no idea she'd just saved his life. She lay low, hoping that there wouldn't be any gunfire.

'Stay down. Stay down. Don't move.' Kirsten felt a gun in her back and a specific instruction to move. She rolled off her man, offering her hands up in surrender.

'That's kilo. That's kilo.' It was Dominic's voice. Kirsten saw the gun being moved away from her face as the man beside her was turned over and his hands tied up behind him with a cable tie. Kirsten continued to lie on the floor, while others moved about above her. It took around thirty seconds before she heard Dominic's voice again. 'This is Delta. All clear, all clear,' and then the lights came back on. Kirsten pulled off her night vision goggles, stood up and looked around her. Eight men were lying on the ground, hands tied behind them, with police officers standing over them, guns still trained.

Kirsten saw the sergeant of the police firearms squad, made her way to him, and announced, 'Good job. Get them out into the truck and we'll take it from there. Thank you.'

The man nodded, gave a brief smile, and then turned around and barked orders at his men. Those who had been gathering to buy a diamond were hauled up and taken from the barn, eventually leaving Kirsten and Dominic inside.

'Any sign yet, Charlie?' asked Kirsten.

It took a few moments before Carrie-Anne came back with it. 'Negative. No one within sight. I think it's a bust.'

Kirsten shook her head and looked at Dominic. 'Someone knew, didn't they?'

'Most likely,' said Dominic. 'There might have been room for a third party here. They talked about it being a bidding war. Maybe the seller was gathering several people. There should have been more than this. Too easy with just a couple. If one side wins, the other doesn't like it, they start to shoot and then grab it. Not good for a seller on his own. I reckon there was meant to be more people here.'

'Well, we'll see,' said Kirsten. 'We might not have what we want, but we have something. We have eight people out there who can spill some beans. Certainly, a bit of discord. Charlie, route back in and we'll get back down to the hold.'

Kirsten was talking about the base back in the centre of Inverness. They didn't have enough room to be able to interrogate eight people there, but instead, they would route via the police station and make sure they kept who they thought were the ringleaders on board before taking the van back to their own base.

'I'll need you to go to the police station and sit in with the basic interviews, is that all right?' Kirsten looked at Dominic as if she'd given him the task of going and getting her team the coffee.

'Of course, it is. You don't have to apologise just because I've been in this job longer than you. You're the boss.'

Kirsten smiled. She was, but she also looked at Dominic, five feet ten, broad-shouldered with a deceptive grin, with a touch of envy. Although he was nearly fifty, and certainly had a haggard look about him, Kirsten had been impressed with how he'd done in the physical side of the tests she had set him. When it came to hand-to-hand fighting, yes, she could probably turn him over, but Dominic could fight dirty, and he'd use everything around him. However, she thought, he'd never get caught in that situation. The man was so streetwise and that's what she wanted—not just as an operative, but someone she could learn off. She felt she was still very green in all of this below the radar work.

A head appeared inside the door of the barn. Kirsten saw Justin Chivers, her communications expert and a man who had an eye for just about every woman going. He was a creep, but when it came to technology, he was the best she'd seen.

'It's time to go,' he said. 'If that's all right, boss.' Kirsten watched him look at her in a way she had seen before. Because she was operating in the field, she had her black cargo trousers on and like her jumper, they were tight and uncompromising, allowing her to move freely but making sure there was nothing loose that could make a noise or hit something on the way. It also seemed to please Justin's eye.

'We'll have less of that,' said Kirsten. 'You're driving.' The man turned away as if he'd been scolded.

'You should make him cut that out. I'm not sure Charlie appreciates it.'

'I don't appreciate it either, but we've all got our foibles and he's too darn good to let go.'

Dominic shrugged his shoulders and made his way out of the barn, followed by Kirsten. Once outside, a police officer closed the doors and sealed them up.

'There'll be two of us here for a while. A couple further out just in case anyone else turns up,' said the officer, 'and then we'll get forensics in. We'll send it along soon as we can, whatever they come up with.'

'Thanks for your help,' shouted Kirsten, while she ran over and jumped into the front of the transit van, where Justin was sitting beside her.

'Good to go, boss?'

Kirsten smiled and looked back at the barn. Well, it hadn't gone perfectly but it wasn't their fault. At least they had something from it. Yes, it was a decent night's work.

'Yes, Justin. Good to go.'

Chapter 2

Kirsten was sitting in the same cargo pants that she'd been wearing up in the rafters of the barn. She had pulled a baggy jumper over her top, not so much to protect herself from the attentions of Justin Chivers but because she was slightly cold. It was now 3:00 a.m. and outside, the Inverness night had turned wet. There was rain on the window, and she looked down into the street beyond, which was quiet. She thought it had been at least thirty minutes since she'd seen a car.

Kirsten was always in a debate as to whether or not to close the curtains. This time of night, it certainly would have been better, and nobody would see what she was doing. On the other hand, she didn't have anything pointed towards the window that was of any value. The trick about staying secret was about knowing when to cover up and when you could be more overt, hiding in plain sight.

She had let Carrie-Anne take care of bringing the two prisoners into the building and they would have been secreted away, one in each interrogation room. They wouldn't hold them for long before they were taken back to the police station and processed through the force's procedures.

There was a knock on the door, and when Kirsten called, 'Come in,' her female colleague approached. Carrie-Anne was Welsh and blonde, and unlike Kirsten, who usually had the image of a fighter, Carrie-Anne looked more like an office clerk. Since they'd come back from the operation, she'd changed into a skirt and blouse and looked every bit the part of office efficiency. Kirsten liked the woman, although she did feel that her hair got paid too much attention. Every time Kirsten looked at her in a free moment, the woman was either playing with it or brushing it. Kirsten felt hair was something to be tied up behind you, so it didn't get in the way or to hide behind when you were feeling sheepish or embarrassed in front of someone you liked. Carrie-Anne wore hers like a peacock wears its feathers.

Kirsten didn't feel that the woman was particularly attractive, having a reasonably large figure, but it was more big-boned than to do with any excess weight and her large frame came into play whenever she had to deal with the physical side of the job. The woman was strong but also well versed in various fighting techniques, so much so that Kirsten actually found her a challenge.

'We're ready, boss,' said Carrie-Anne, and Kirsten looked up at her.

'We really have to change that. I know I'm the boss but it's Kirsten. I'm not working that sort of team.'

'Sorry,' said Carrie-Anne. 'It's just that's what the old boss wanted. He quite liked it when I told him he was the boss.'

'I bet he did, and I bet you used it when you wanted to get somewhere. I don't see you as the subservient type of woman.'

Carrie-Anne laughed. 'Yes. Fell for it every time. You'd think being a spy, he would have a better idea of when I was turning it on and turning it off.'

Kirsten grinned. 'Let's get in here, then. Time to turn it on with these guys.'

Kirsten led the way down a flight of stairs into the rear room of the building where a man sat on the far side of the desk. His hands were handcuffed through a strong fixture in the desk and there were lights shining on him. Kirsten sat down in a seat that meant his view was obscured by the bright lights behind her.

'What were you after tonight?' asked Kirsten.

'Don't you set a tape going or something?' said the man.

'That will be done,' said Kirsten, 'but if I want your voice recorded, I'll record it. It's not a problem. Answer the question.'

The man shook his head. 'I want a lawyer in here.'

'Your lawyer comes later. At the moment, you're just being transported in the van back to the police. I need you to tell me what's going on.'

'What do you mean what's going on? It was just a gang meeting. Things to talk about.'

'I was in the rafters for five hours beforehand. You're not telling me that,' said Kirsten.

Carrie-Anne stepped forward, made her way round to the side of the desk that the man was sitting on. She hopped up onto the desk, letting her thigh touch the man's arm. Kirsten could see the man react gently, almost smiling at the Welsh woman in front of him. And then she reached out with her hand, taking him by the throat.

'We haven't got time for this. You can sit and mess about with the police all you want. She asked what you were there for. You tell us what's going on and you'll be back with the police, you'll be processed, you'll probably be out on the street in a couple of hours. After all, what have you done? Not a lot. You might get done with firearms. Have you got a licence for that thing? No, I didn't think so but if we don't know what's going on, you won't be going back to them. We'll investigate the terrorist plot that was going on.'

The man looked up, shocked, but he struggled to speak because of Carrie-Anne's hand on his throat. 'There's no terrorist plot,' he said. 'We're not terrorists.'

'Tell us what happened,' said Kirsten. 'What were you there for? We know your seller didn't arrive. Auction, was it?'

'Let me go and I'll say.'

Carrie-Anne let her hand slip, but she stayed close to the man.

'It was an auction. There are diamonds on the go. Apparently, the price was quite good. They said somebody else wants them.'

'What do you mean?' asked Kirsten. 'Somebody else wants them.'

'The way I got told it,' said the man, 'was that there were these diamonds coming in and if we got hold of them we could get a better price, so the guy who was selling them, he was going to come and drop them to us and then we were going to sell them on.'

'Who are you selling them on to?' asked Kirsten.

'Only have a name, he was called Gustav. Communication wasn't great. He said we were to meet him at a hotel tomorrow.'

'Which hotel?' asked Kirsten.

'Royal Hotel, Cromarty. Do you know it?'

'Of course, I know it,' said Kirsten. 'When are you meant to meet him?'

'Lunchtime.'

'And he's the one that gave you the detail?' said Kirsten. The man nodded. 'And what detail was it?'

'Well, he said there was things I weren't to say.'

'Like what?' asked Kirsten. The man shook his head and turned away. Carrie-Anne reached out again with a hand taking him by the throat and applying a lot of pressure.

'I told you I can't say.'

'I think it's time to talk,' said Carrie-Anne, and with that, she jumped off the table, made her way around the man and wrapped her arm around his neck. This time she squeezed hard. Kirsten could see the sleeper hold she was putting on him. It wouldn't kill him. Instead, it would eventually just knock him out, but he didn't know that.

'Okay,' said the man, gasping. 'Gustav said they were for a foreign person. Some other country.'

'Foreign country. Which one?' asked Kirsten.

'He didn't say, I think it's Arab though. They like all the diamonds and that, don't they?'

'People all over the world like diamonds,' said Carrie-Anne. 'You sure you can't be more specific?' and she wrapped the arm around his neck again.

'No,' said the man quickly. 'I can't. He didn't say. Gustav said turn up here, bid this, get the diamonds, bring them to the hotel, and then I would get a cut of what he was getting paid.'

'What was your cut to be?'

'Ten percent,' said the man, 'but Gustav said that we'd probably be in the millions.'

'In the millions at ten percent?' said Carrie-Anne. 'What sort of diamonds were these?'

'I don't know. I don't know.'

Kirsten nodded to Carrie-Anne, and she let the man's neck go. Together the women left, leaving the man in his room alone with the light still pouring down on him. Moving to the next room, Kirsten found a thinner man who was sweating, and looking extremely agitated.

'Why am I here? Why am I not down with the police?'

'Do you know what you walked into?' asked Kirsten. The man's eyes watched as Carrie-Anne moved up beside him.

'The lady wanted an answer,' said Carrie-Anne.

'I was just there. They simply told me to go and buy something. All right?'

'You came with guns, and you got agitated, and things nearly kicked off before we came in.'

'That's right,' said Carrie-Anne. 'You owe us one. Really, you'd be dead if it wasn't for us. Who was this guy you were working for?'

'Don't know. Just got a contact.'

'And he wants you to meet him, does he? How were you going to get the diamonds to him?'

'He said he'd come to me. Said I should collect them, and he'd come to me.'

'What, you just did that? You had somebody say, "Go here, pick up these diamonds, take the gun with you," and you just did it,' said Kirsten.

'This one doesn't sound very clever,' said Carrie-Anne.

'He gave me the money up front.'

'How much?' asked Kirsten.

'Fifty thousand. He gave me fifty thousand up front. Said there'd be much more afterwards.'

'Looks like you're giving the fifty thousand back,' said Kirsten.

She looked over at Carrie-Anne, who smirked down at the man, but they both knew that the man's contact would probably never come to him again. If they were paying that much money, they'd be watching him return home, and when he came empty handed, they would scarper.

'What else do you know?' asked Kirsten.

'Well, there's diamonds. It's all diamonds they want.'

'Diamonds have names,' said Carrie-Anne. 'Did you know that? Some of the best diamonds have names. Do you know any diamond names?'

'Names?' said the man. 'No, I don't.'

'Did you know any of the names of these diamonds?'

'No. He just said I was to pick them up.'

'How did you know you were going to buy the right things?' asked Kirsten.

'Because he said it was in a bag and the bag would be decorated.'

'How was the bag decorated?'

'He said it would be lilac, lilac with orange pansies on it.'

'Do you know what pansies look like?' asked Carrie-Anne.

'They're flowers, aren't they?' said the man. 'It's got orange flowers on it. Lilac. That's like purple, isn't it?'

Kirsten started wondering to herself what was going on. *These two men, were they being used by the same person, or were there two different groups? Why were they so keen to get the diamonds? More than that, why were they so keen to use other people? Maybe it was because they would stand out, especially if they were foreigners. It was funny like that. You could possibly go to America from Scotland, change your accent, and you might fit in, but could you be an American if you came from China? Yes, there were Chinese people in America, but their ways were different, weren't they? Harder to match up to the cultural norms. In the Middle East as well. Maybe they would struggle. The other man had mentioned the Middle East.*

Kirsten spent another ten minutes with the man, but he was giving everything up so readily it was quite clear he didn't even know that much. When she stepped out of the room, Carrie-Anne followed, and she led her back up to her office, where she found Dominic inside.

'They're going to do more of the police interviews in the morning, letting people sleep.'

'That's all right. I think we've got what we want,' said Kirsten. 'And I've got a job for you tomorrow. There's a meet in the Royal Hotel in Cromarty, a man called Gustav. If you go down to the subject in number one, he'll give you a description. I need you to go and meet Gustav as he apparently set them up to buy the diamonds. We need to find out what these diamonds are because this is all over the top.'

'Not a problem, boss,' said Dominic, and Kirsten gave him a look.

'I told Carrie-Anne that's not what we say. It's Kirsten in here.'

'Kirsten, boss,' said Dominic.

'Now, I said I don't want boss.'

'But you are,' said Dominic. 'I know what you want, but we're not used to it, and frankly, I don't want to get to saying your name out loud all the time. Too easy for it to slip out instead of Kilo.'

Kirsten nodded. Maybe there were some things she'd have to compromise on. She'd gone through her time in the police where she saw her former leader Seoras Macleod having to change from being called boss to being called Seoras, and he hated it. Lost the formality, he had thought, for a familiarity that was dangerous. Maybe Dominic was right. She watched as the man left the room, and then remembered that Carrie-Anne was still there. The woman had an ability to almost lurk without being noticed.

'You're on the bag tomorrow. I know it's not much to go on, but we need to try and dig it up. Get hold of Justin, see if anything's come across any of the wires, see if there's any word out there about it. Maybe you two can hunt down the seller as we still have no idea who he is.'

'Okay, I'll let Dominic talk to these guys then I get them back to the police. After that, I'm going to grab a couple of hours, if that's okay.'

'Of course,' said Kirsten. 'You going home, or are you using the room up here?'

'I'll use the room here. It's not worth going home, is it?'

It's not, thought Kirsten. *It's not, but that's a really bad habit to get into.* 'If that's the case,' she said, 'I'm going to go head home now. I'll be back here by eight o'clock in the morning.'

With that, Kirsten grabbed her stuff and made her way out of the building. She drove her car back home, fell into her flat, and hauled off the baggy jumper she'd put on at work. She thought about just slipping into the bed, because at best she'd maybe get three or four hours' sleep, but she stank. It had been hard maintaining that height for five hours in the rafters. Then they'd gone through all the drama and like anyone normal, she sweated. Kirsten stripped off, made her way into the shower and let the water fall over her, soaking away the energies of the night. When she stepped out, she quickly dried herself and fell into bed. As she lay there, her mind was on two things.

Firstly, there was the case. A lilac bag, a man called Gustav, and a seller they didn't know. Who these people were, what they would be doing, and how to catch them tumbled through her mind, but there was something else here. Something else going on that bothered her. Something that had never bothered her before.

With her rise in the ranks and the increased money she was now due, she'd bought herself a new bed and it was a large one, a double. Her arms reached out in front of her, and she felt someone should be filling that space. With the life she now led, it seemed that she got out less and less. Even going to the gym was hard. She was now the boss of the team and so she didn't fraternise the same way. She felt she needed someone close, someone to talk to. Just someone. Kirsten fell asleep, her mind not knowing who that person could be.

Chapter 3

John hated these days. They were trying to cram half a round extra in, and it meant being on your feet for longer. And to top all that, the rain was pelting down. True, he had the workwear, leggings, boots, and jacket, along with a beanie on his head which at least kept him warm. The gloves he wore to prevent picking up any contamination that was left in the bins, but as he marched along behind the yellow wagon, grabbing the handles of the mid-chest high black receptacles, John was not in a good mood.

He pulled a couple of the bins across, put them onto the back of the wagon, and then pressed the button for the platforms to lift them up and tip them relentlessly into the back of the van. Once the mechanism kicked twice, thereby dumping all of the rubbish, it brought the bins back down and John would make his trip back to wherever he'd picked them up from, back and forward, back and forward. Most days, this didn't bother John, but today was an early start, six in the morning, and it would be a six o'clock finish this evening.

The rain had already got going, and now, at almost seven o'clock, John thought he might start to see daylight breaking through. They weren't allowed to start before six o'clock, as they made too much noise, but these days in Inverness, a lot of people were on the move in the early morning. The city had grown from what John had known of it as a boy and now it was busy and bustling nearly all of the time.

John lived on a suburban estate and as he looked at the posh houses he couldn't afford, John felt even lower. Most of these bins would have been left out the night before, after the council had put out information the previous week saying that the bins would be collected earlier, and John had already found a few that had been knocked over or blown down in the wind. It was so much better if they put them out just before John arrived.

The bin men reached the end of the street and John jumped into the wagon as it was driven around the corner before stopping again, forcing him back out into the rain. He stepped out to grab the black bin in front of him. It felt heavy. *What'd they put in this?* he thought, but he applied his foot to the base of it, grabbed the handles and tipped it towards himself, before wheeling it towards the bin lorry. It was a bit of a push to get it onto the platform to lift up. John then pressed the button, happy to see it disappear. It would be lighter on the return trip.

Up it went. It kicked hard once. It kicked hard twice, but John didn't hear things falling out properly. He pressed the button again, forcing the bin to jar, hoping that whatever inside would now disappear down and into the lorry. When it didn't do so, John pressed a button that would lower the mechanism so he could have a look inside.

That was the trouble these days, people put just about anything in their bins. Who knew what it was? Once there was a foot spa so wide it had jammed inside the bin. It was electrical. What was it doing in the bin, anyway? It should have been taken to the dump or the recycling facility as it was now called. But people were lazy, of which John was only too aware, so time and again, they found bizarre things inside the bins.

He threw back the lid and peered inside. At first, he struggled to see what was there, for it was still dark outside and they were quite a distance from a streetlight. He reached down, but with his gloved hand, he struggled to understand what he was feeling. There was some sort of hair. Maybe it was one of those toy dogs, large and stuffed, that had blocked the bin on the way down. He reached and tried to pull it, but it was heavy, and so he went round to the front of the van where Len, the driver, gave him a wide frown.

'What's up?'

'Just a stuck bin, Len. I can't see what it is, though. Have you got the torch in there?'

'Yeah, here you go,' said Len. 'Just give us a shout if you need me to give you a hand.'

John nodded. He plodded his way back round to the rear of the lorry where Andrew, who was out pulling the bins along with John, had now made his way over to see what was happening. In fairness, you didn't get a lot of laughs on this job, and you certainly didn't get a lot of entertainment from what was inside the bin, so when something happened it was worth having a look, because it may be the only funny thing that day.

Andrew looked down. 'I can't see much. Can you?'

'Get out of the way,' said John, and produced the torch. Clicking the beam of light on, he shone it inside the bin and then recoiled.

'What's up?' asked Andrew.

'I thought I saw a head down there.'

'Oh, it's probably one of those Halloween things.'

John nodded and put his torch back down. 'Here,' he said to Andrew, 'you reach down and grab it. It looks like some sort of mannequin or dummy.'

Andrew reached in, but with two hands he was unable to lift up the figure. John joined him and together they started to raise up the heavy load inside. As it reached the top of the bin, Andrew screamed. It had suddenly become clear that this was no mannequin, but a body. The left eye socket was blown out, half the face torn away, leaving no doubt about how the person had died. Andrew dropped the body, causing John to stumble forward, his grip still sure, before letting go. Andrew, falling back, tripped, hitting his head on the pavement, making him cry out in pain. As he put his hand up to his head, he could feel something pouring out.

'I've been cut. There's blood,' said Andrew.

'What do you mean?' said John, his eyes disbelieving, still looking back to the bin.

'Look,' said Andrew, 'look.' He held his hand forward and John could see a dark stain that he assumed was blood.

Len had jumped out of the front of the wagon and was coming round to the rear. 'What's the matter?' he asked. 'What's going on?'

'There's a body in there, Len, a body. Call them.'

'Who?' asked Len.

'Police,' said John.

'And a bloody ambulance,' said Andrew. 'Cut my head.'

John watched Andrew fiddling away with the back of his head and then saw Len sprint for the front of the cab. Something inside John made him step forward and look once more into that bin. He shone the torch inside and looking back up at him was a single eye, bemoaning the lack of its twin.

* * *

Kirsten was arriving at her office, and on hearing the ringing from her desk, she picked up the phone.

'Kirsten, it's Justin. Just had a call from the police station. It's a routine thing, saying they'd found a dead body in a bin, but it wasn't that far from last night's barn. Just wondering if you wanted to take a call over, see if it's anything we need to look at.'

'Isn't Dominic out that way, or Carrie-Anne?'

'Dominic's headed off towards Cromarty already. Said he wanted to do some snooping around to see if anyone arrives early. Carrie-Anne's a no show yet. I just thought as you were probably not far from it, it might be easier for you just to pop out and decide it's nothing.'

Kirsten realised Justin would do anything not to inconvenience Carrie-Anne. Much as it was clear that the woman detested him, Justin was always ever hopeful, believing himself to be God's gift to women.

'Okay. I'm heading back out that way. You keep me posted on anything else.'

'Will do, boss,' said Justin, saying the word as if it was most ridiculous statement ever made.

Kirsten drove back towards the barn she'd been in the previous night but cut off towards a suburban area and pulled up outside a house, having followed the address in a text from Justin. As she came close, she saw a police cordon, a yellow bin lorry sitting close by and a friendly face she knew from her past.

'Well, look who it is. What on earth are you doing here?'

Kirsten held her hand up as she got out of the car and waved over to Detective Sergeant Hope McGrath. Hope had been Kirsten's boss, her line manager, sitting in between herself and Inspector Macleod, and she had a real like for the six-foot, red-haired woman.

'Where's the boss?' asked Kirsten.

'Oh, he'll be along soon enough,' said Hope. 'I just got here first to see if it there was anything that needed doing quickly. He was out late last night.'

'Is he okay?' asked Kirsten. She'd always felt that Macleod had given her a boost in her career, elevated her up from being a street bobby into a detective, and she was eternally grateful to him. It was that and the fact that he had visited her brother when she couldn't at the residential home where he had to stay because of his dementia.

'He's fine. Same old Seoras.'

'What have we got?' asked Kirsten.

'Dead body in the bin,' said Hope, 'but why are you here?'

'We had an incident close to here last night with someone who didn't show; we were just wondering if this could be something to do with it.'

'Okay,' said Hope. 'Is that all the detail I get these days?'

'I'm afraid so,' said Kirsten. 'Except one thing I can tell you is that he may have had a bag with him, lilac with orange pansies apparently.'

'A real man's man, then,' said Hope, laughing. 'But funny enough, you may be in luck,' she said. 'Put on a suit, Jona's on scene.'

Jona Nakamura was the senior forensic officer at Inverness

Police Station and Hope McGrath led Kirsten over to their scenes-of-crime vehicle where they both donned suits and made their way back to watch the bin that was still sitting at the rear of the lorry.

'How far have you got on, Jona?' asked Hope.

'Oh,' said Jona. 'Kirsten, how are things?'

'Good, Jona. Hope says you've might have one for me here. Got a bag with him?'

'Yes,' said Jona. 'We've taken fingerprints of the man. I'm running them through at the moment to see if we can identify him. There's ID inside but we believe it to be false. Cheaply made, by the looks of it as well.'

'But the bag,' said Kirsten. 'Have you got it?'

'I fished it out,' said Jona, and waved them over back to the scenes-of-crime vehicle, where she opened the back door and let them inside up towards the front cab. On a shelf at the side, Jona removed the bag and placed it in front of Kirsten. 'As long as you keep it inside the plastic, you're welcome to handle it,' said Jona. 'If you want to take it out, let me know and I'll open it for you.'

'What's this about then?' said Hope.

'Possible carrier, not doing what he was supposed to and paid for it or got ambushed by somebody else. We believe he may have been making a sale last night, different parties involved. We broke it up, but we waited for him to arrive first of all and he never showed. We don't know much else because we got it on the wiretaps. It's quite hush-hush, Hope. There might be a foreign interest as well. It wouldn't surprise me if we take this one from you.'

'It's a body in a bin,' said Hope. 'It's not the most glamorous case in the world. You can have it.'

'I'm not sure Macleod will see it that way,' laughed Kirsten. 'Was there anything else on the body, Jona?'

'Well, here's the ID he had,' said Jona, taking another plastic bag off a shelf and passing it to Kirsten. She glanced at it. 'Piers Smith, but if you look at it,' said Jona, 'it's a cheap copy. Hasn't got the correct watermarks, hasn't got the correct threads running through it. I mean, it's a false passport all the way. You'd have to be showing that to a complete idiot on a border control.'

'So, you're saying he may have entered some other way or is he from here?'

'I don't know at the moment,' said Jona. 'I'll try and find out for you.' The pair returned to the dustbin, and with gloves on, Kirsten looked inside and tilted the body up so she could see the man's face.

'Yes, it's nice, isn't it?' said Hope.

'Gun up to the face, almost blew the side of his head off. Significant damage to the brain,' Jona said. 'Instantaneous death. Cobbled together and put in here, so somewhere there's a crime scene that we haven't found yet.'

'And you won't find it. That looks like a proper hit,' said Kirsten.

'I did realise that,' said Hope, 'but you know how good the old man is.'

'Like I say, I don't think the old man's going to get to know about this.' Kirsten stayed talking with Hope for another couple of minutes before she heard a cry from the forensic vehicle. Jona was waving them over again.

'Just got a hit from the fingerprints. That's from Interpol, though. Appears that the guy's a well-known fence on the continent. A Franz Huber.'

'Who's the contact at Interpol?' asked Kirsten and Jona noted it down for her. 'Well, anyway, I need to run this back through my people. We may be taking this one off you but that's good work, Jona,' said Kirsten. 'We've got a name for the body anyway. And with the bag, it ties up to the guy we were waiting for.'

'Just let me know as soon as,' said Hope. 'I'm not doing all this work for you to get no reward.' She punched Kirsten on the shoulder. The pair laughed and as Kirsten went to walk away Hope called her. 'What's with the hair? It's not quite red, is it? But heading towards it. What was wrong with your original colour?'

'Get seen too often these days. My hair colour changes like the chief of police. New one for every season.'

She saw Hope smirk, and Kirsten made her way back to her own car.

'By the way,' shouted Hope. 'It's good if you take this soon because I'm meant to be going on a cruise.'

'A cruise?' queried Kirsten.

'Yes,' said Hope. 'Biggest cruise ship in the world's coming this way. *Her Majesty's Pride.* She's doing trials. Managed to wangle in to be a pretend passenger or whatever they call it. People who check the service out. She's routing her way up into Aberdeen, then a trip to Shetland and round to Stornoway. Very local but I'll get on it for a couple of days. I have to do a bit of a review and that. But I won't get there if you don't take this case off us. You know what Macleod's like. He won't want me to go.'

'You're entitled to your leave,' said Kirsten. 'I take it you've still got Ross with you?'

'Like Ross is ever going to leave. We've also got a new one

with us, though. Right feisty. Takes on Macleod in a way you never could.'

Or ever wanted to, thought Kirsten. But she smiled, gave a wave and stepped inside her car. Kirsten picked up her mobile, calling Justin Chivers and relaying the details, asking him to make a connection with Interpol. As soon as she put the call down, her mobile rang again, and she saw it was Anna Hunt.

'Kirsten, I need you in London now.'

'Excuse me?' said Kirsten. 'I've just picked up detail on a case. We might be able to track down our mystery seller from last night.'

'Good,' said Anna, 'but I need you in London.'

'Why?' asked Kirsten.

'I said I need you in London,' said Anna. 'I'm not telling you why, I'm telling you to get to London. I believe you can be here out of Inverness around about four in the afternoon. I'll send a car to pick you up from Gatwick.'

'Okay,' said Kirsten. 'I'll go book the flight.'

'No, you won't,' said Anna. 'The details will be coming through on your phone. Go sort out your team, get changed, get down here. And look the part, okay? You're going to meet somebody important.'

The phone call went dead. Kirsten sat looking at the phone for a while. Anna never spoke like that. *Look the part?* She found that bizarre. Kirsten also didn't like getting dressed up. She tolerated wearing skirts and blazers and jackets for interviews. Outside of that, she really didn't want to bother.

She picked up the phone, calling back Justin Chivers.

'Justin, it appears I'm off to London. Can you call the team and just make sure that they're on top of things? Tell them I'll be off the grid for a while. Got the feeling Anna wants to take me somewhere where not a lot of people will know.'

'That's understood,' said Justin. 'By the way, your tickets have just come through on your email.'

Kirsten shook her head. Off to London it was.

Chapter 4

Kirsten sat in the emergency exit row during the flight down to London. She had ordered a coffee and was stretching her feet out but in truth, she was feeling distinctly uncomfortable. She wore a black jacket over a white blouse with a trim skirt that ran down to her knees, but beyond that, it got complicated. Kirsten liked to wear hiking boots or trainers, but they obviously wouldn't have gone with the outfit. She detested heels, especially high ones that stopped her from running. In her current job, she never knew when she would have to sprint.

Anna once had seen her wear a pair of black low-heeled shoes and chastised her for it, telling her she needed to use every ounce of femininity she could at times. Her boss certainly knew how to turn on the charm when she wanted to, though Kirsten was well aware she was in control of it. In her bag, above her in the locker, was a pair of trainers but on Kirsten's feet were a set of high heels that made her feel like she was three inches taller than she should be. She had spent twenty minutes brushing her hair out, something else she rarely did, certainly not in the middle of the day. She'd also showered once again before heading off.

Still, she'd almost slapped Justin Chivers for the look he gave her. 'You can really wear the stuff when you want to,' he had said. It was fine. Kirsten had taken that as a compliment, but when he mentioned about her legs doing something to every man, it was a step too far and instead of punching him, she simply stepped forward, and placed her sharp heel onto his toe.

The flight down was giving her time to reflect, and she was wondering why she was making her way here. *Anna had said that it was good that she had an ID on her seller so was this going to be connected?* So far, in Kirsten's short career, Anna had never summoned her down to London. She was used to Anna being around Glasgow, Edinburgh, popping down occasionally for briefings, but never this urgent, this unplanned, and never had her flight been booked for her. As she stepped through the concourse at Gatwick, Kirsten made her way down to the drop-off spot where she saw a Jaguar pull up beside her and the passenger door opening.

'Miss Kirsten Stewart,' said a man leaning over with a trim cap on his head. 'My name is Johnson. Miss Hunt has sent me for you.'

Kirsten bent down fighting against her skirt to do so, but she wanted to see the eyes of the man inside. He did look like a driver. He certainly didn't seem to be a threat, but that was not how you did things.

'Designation and code?' asked Kirsten. The man stated, 'Driver,' and then gave an eight-digit code which Kirsten had been sent previously, allowing her to identify her pickup. Satisfied the man knew it, she made her way around to the boot of the vehicle trying to open it before the man raced out to take her luggage. He placed it in the boot before shutting it and escorting her back round to the passenger seat. Once she was inside, he made his way back round to the driver's side.

'If you want to say you're a driver, you're going to have to do better than that,' said Kirsten.

'Yes, ma'am.'

'And you never address me as ma'am.'

'Well, actually, if I'm a driver and you're a pick-up, I think I should, but, yes, I did make a mistake in throwing the door open for you.'

Kirsten smirked, looked across again at the man who seemed to be around his mid-twenties. His eyes flicked round to her a couple of times, but, generally, he kept them on the road. He did seem somewhat nervous though.

'Where are we going?' asked Kirsten.

'I can't say.'

'Good. You haven't been in this game long though, have you?'

'No, I haven't, but Miss Hunt distinctly said that you were not to know where you were going.'

'And whom am I meeting?'

'Miss Hunt,' said the man, 'as far as I know.' He fixed his eyes back on the road. They stayed in silence as Johnson drove along, but Kirsten caught the man turning and staring at her every now and again. Being the age he was, and Kirsten being not that much older, she was taking this as a compliment for he didn't seem to leer, just to be in a little bit of wonder at her.

'What's the matter? The road not good enough for you?' she said. She watched the man panic, fixing his eyes back on the road.

'I'm sorry. It's just that—'

Kirsten felt sorry for him. She'd been a bit rough on teasing him like that.

'It's just what?'

'Well, you stopped that gunman, didn't you? Stopped him shooting the First Minister? You were the one who helped Anna bring down the traitors inside as well. Your name is pretty big down here.'

'My name?'

'Well, amongst the operatives. I mean, I didn't know your actual name, not until I was told to pick you up but you're doing well up there, aren't you?'

'I'm doing my job,' said Kirsten. 'Can we keep going?'

'Sorry,' he said, 'you did ask.'

'I did,' said Kirsten, 'but I think we've said enough. Let's get to where we're going.'

Kirsten always felt a bit uneasy in a spy game. If she had been in the police force, she'd have talked away to the man, happily told her about what was going on. When she looked at him, he seemed a decent sort, and in fairness, he was fairly attractive. She thought back to lying in the bed, part of her thinking, *what it would be like to have this man lying beside her? Focus,* she thought, *just focus.*

They arrived at a park somewhere outside of Gatwick and Kirsten was asked to get out of the car while her driver drove off. He had left her at a small bench, and she sat down trying her best to decide whether to cross her legs over or keep them side by side in the skirt. She never had these issues normally, always in trousers. She decided that she would cross her legs and leaned back into the wooden bench, allowing her shoulders to just sit against the top. Shortly after, another car pulled up and Anna Hunt stepped out holding open the door. This was no small Jaguar, but rather a large limousine with dark windows.

'Good to see you, Kirsten,' said Anna, 'and looking so well. Inside, please.'

Kirsten nodded, stepped inside the rear of the limousine, and saw a man sitting in the rearmost seat. There was a seat facing him and Kirsten was offered it by the man's simple hand gesture. Anna followed her in and together, the two women sat looking at the man opposite. He had grey hair but what there was, was neatly cut, and he had a pleasant face, if somewhat narrow. Kirsten reckoned he must have been in his seventies.

The man reached forward offering a hand. 'Hello, Miss Stewart, Miss Hunt here has told me great things about you. It's a delight to meet you. My name is Godfrey.'

Kirsten waited for a surname, but none came. 'Pleased to meet you as well,' said Kirsten. 'Forgive me for I'm not as refined as Anna is.'

'No,' said Godfrey, in surprise, 'but you certainly look the part and we've been hearing great things that you've done. Nice work, by the way, saving our First Minister. There may be some political people down here who wouldn't have minded her being bumped off, but as government officials, we seek the protection of all politicians.' Kirsten almost laughed for she saw the wry smile coming from the man's lips. 'I'm afraid, my dear, you've stumbled upon a rather serious situation. I've been told that you almost apprehended the seller of certain diamonds last night, up in the Inverness area.'

'I did,' said Kirsten. 'Well, unfortunately, he's now dead. Stuck in a bin on the edge of Inverness. Shot in the face. It was a proper hit, Godfrey.'

'Godfrey is well aware of the whole situation,' said Anna, 'I have briefed him on it.'

'Indeed, I am,' said Godfrey, 'and I'm aware of a lot more, but something you need to be aware of is that one of the foreign powers in the Middle East—actually, I'm not at liberty to mention them by name—has had a particular gemstone taken. It has a name in Arabic but in English, it's known as the *Light of the World*. It's large and about this size.'

Godfrey held up his hand spreading his fingers about ten centimetres apart.

'What it really does is glisten. If you look at it, there's a slight gleam of green to it inside which is a taint but it's a taint that's seen in a different light by certain people. The country in question sees the theft of it as something of national importance and certainly national pride, and they're very aware it's in the UK. We are reliant on this country for certain military installations in the Middle East area but our problem is that although they are a small country, they are preparing to take matters into their own hands to recover this gem.'

'So, you're saying we need to find it?' said Kirsten.

'Exactly, my dear, and you'll need to find it within the next week, possibly a lot quicker. I'm not sure how long we can hold them off for. We have reached out, through various sources, and we too were able to clarify it was in the north of Scotland. However, it was only your intelligence that made us believe it might have been this particular seller. We know now that his name is Huber, and we believe he brought the diamond through a week ago.

'He's been gathering up potential customers using other fences, but we think someone's now taken it and disposed of him. You need to be aware, Miss Stewart, that the government wants this handled quietly and quickly. There's more than one interested party here. The country it was stolen from, they want it back quickly, and we believe they're already operating in this country. Understand that if you have it, they may use force to take it off you and they'll certainly use force to take it off other people.

'We have stated to them that if we find it, we will give it back to them, and obviously said that they shouldn't work against us. To which point they said, they weren't working in the country. It's a downright lie but let's face it, we would do the same in their place. The other problem is, they have a rival. Another Arab country that would love to rub their face in this one. They'll be in Scotland trying to buy it as well, and if you throw on top of that, the various collectors around the world who know what a piece this is, there's no end of buyers. We believe Mr. Huber was holding out, trying to drum up the business, as they say, looking to get the best price. It's kind of backfired on him.'

'You can say that again.' Kirsten looked out of the tinted windows and noticed that they were driving past, time and again, the same view.

'I see you haven't been in a car like this before,' said Godfrey. 'You need to understand that these things are so very sensitive. We don't take them inside an office. We don't take them anywhere. This is the only briefing you'll get. The only person who knows what you know now, are me, a couple of people at the highest level of intelligence, the Prime Minister, and Miss Hunt here, and it stays that way.'

'Are you clear on everything?' asked Anna.

'I think so,' said Kirsten, 'get the diamond, give it back.'

'Exactly,' said Godfrey, 'find it and understand that you have authorisation to use lethal force to achieve our aim but obviously don't make a scene.'

'Keep it quiet. It's always the best way,' said Anna, 'I'm on the end of the phone if you need me. I shall be keeping in constant contact with London. If the situation develops, I'll advise you. In the meantime, your flight's booked back up tonight.'

'There isn't another flight up,' said Kirsten.

'When you step out of this car, wait on the bench. The young gentleman that picked you up at Gatwick will pick you up again. There's an ambulance flight flying up from Northolt to Inverness tonight, poor soul returning home for his last days. They were going to have to send him up by ambulance which given his state was not going to happen. Fortunately, we were able to help. They'll get you back up quickly.'

Godfrey leaned forward as the car was being brought to a halt. 'Thank you, Miss Stewart,' he said. 'Best of British to you. Remember, we need to handle this and without a lot of fuss.'

'Understood,' said Kirsten, and as Anna opened the door, she stepped out pulling her skirt down and fixing it before taking a seat on the bench. Anna followed her out of the car.

'In the big time now,' said Anna. 'Try not to make a mistake. I mean it, if you need me, but you know that territory up there better than anyone, as does Justin, so use him, find out what we need to know. Morning or night, you can contact me with any reasonable update.'

Kirsten nodded after being wished good luck by Anna. She watched the woman step back inside the limousine and it drove off. Thirty seconds later, the Jaguar pulled up again.

This time the man stepped out, walked around to the far side, and opened the door for Kirsten to get inside but she continued to sit. 'Just need to make a phone call if you don't mind. Take a seat beside me.'

Kirsten picked up her mobile and rang Dominic.

'This is Dominic,' he said.

'How did it go this afternoon?'

'Not well. Gustav showed up but he made me. In saying that, it wasn't that difficult, there wasn't anybody else about. I think he'd already got wind and was just taking a gander to see what was going on so I'm afraid that's a dead end. I hear we've had luck with a bag.'

'We have indeed but somebody's on the move,' said Kirsten. 'I'll speak to you when I'm back up. Should be there by tonight so don't leave the base until I'm back. That goes for everyone. I need a conference with you all.'

'Will do,' and the call was closed.

Kirsten turned and looked at the driver beside her. 'What time's the flight?'

'Well, they gave you a window, so you've probably got a couple of hours.'

'Good,' said Kirsten. 'Do you like coffee?' The man looked at her blankly. I said, 'Do you like coffee?'

'Well, I do drink a lot of the stuff,' said the man.

'Well, you'll do me then,' said Kirsten. 'Let's get in the car. I want you to take me somewhere nice, somewhere with a bit of a view and I want you to tell me about somewhere you've been, somewhere I can ask you about. I don't mean within the business.'

The man looked at her. 'What?' asked Kirsten.

'It's a bit strange, isn't it?' The man said. 'Why do you want me to do that?'

'The longer you get into this game, and I'm not that long in,' said Kirsten, 'it starts to get lonely. I'm not James Bond and I'm not taking you to bed,' she said. 'Just be nice to have a chat with someone, talk about nothing. You think you can do that?'

Kirsten caught Johnson's eyes quickly weighing her up.

'If you like,' he said. He stood up and held open the door of the car for her. Kirsten looked at him. *He's down here in London. What a waste*, she thought. *Still, let's enjoy ourselves for a couple of hours.* She stepped into the car and gave the man the biggest smile he'd probably had that day. There was plenty of time for work later on.

Chapter 5

Dominic Fields stepped off the bus and hurriedly made his way through the rain inside the large shopping centre located in the middle of Inverness. Walking quickly, he made his way to the central set of escalators before backtracking on his route, except one floor above. It was approximately twenty minutes ago he had picked up a tail. He was unsure what the person was doing, unaware of any reason for him to be tailed but it was definitely a tail. The person had followed Dominic on a merry parade of jumping on and off three buses and then walking a crazy path to the centre of town. Anyone else coming into the shopping centre surely wouldn't have climbed up to the first floor then take the stairs back down and leave by the rear exit, but this man had. Dominic could lose him; that was the long and short of it, but he was more interested in why this person was following him.

Making his way out of town and into the residential streets of Inverness, Dominic climbed a large hill, passing traffic lights before turning left into what was a rather more sedate road. Yes, there was a car every minute or so but generally, this was a residential area of houses that spoke of money. Dominic appeared to not have a care in the world marching along, his rucksack over his shoulder. He was scanning, however, each side of the road looking for the perfect house and about halfway along he spied it.

The house was a large decadent affair but had a short driveway leading to it with large trees on either side. Once he cut in, Dominic would not be seen. If the person following him was wanting to check if he was going to enter into the house, they would have to take a risk, jump around the corner before they were sure Dominic was away. Given how easy the tail was to spot behind him, Dominic reckoned that the guy would fall for the bait.

He turned left, took two steps, and moved close to one of the trees that lined the driveway. He crouched down, making sure the wall that accompanied the trees between the houses sheltered him from any eyes, and then Dominic waited.

He first saw a head peering around the corner of the trees. Then a couple of feet stepping forward. It was the same man, six feet four, which is never a good thing for somebody trying to tail someone else, and certainly built well, but Dominic wasn't going to give him a chance to lay any hands on him. As the man stepped past Dominic, unaware of him within the trees, Dominic made his move, coming around behind the man and reaching around with this tie, throttling the man and pulling him into the trees. He kicked at the man's knees which caused him to fall, landing on his backside. Still, Dominic throttled him from behind. The man's hands went up.

'Now, now,' said Dominic, 'less of that. Why are you following me?'

'I'm not following you.' The man fought to get out, but Dominic squeezed tighter.

'There's no need to lie to me. I know you've been following

me. I've watched you the whole way. Why? What's the point of following me? Who sent you?' The man's hands shot up again, but Dominic pulled tighter.

'I'll keep it at this level if you keep your hands down. You lift them higher and I'll constrict tighter. Soon you'll pass out, and I'll take you somewhere where we can interrogate you properly; do you understand me?' There was a faint movement of the man's head indicating that he did. 'If you want to walk away, son, start talking. Who sent you?'

'Davidson,' he said. 'Mr. Davidson sent me.'

'Carl Davidson?'

'Yes, Carl Davidson. I do a little work for him. Sort some things out.'

Dominic could believe this man was sent on errands by Carl Davidson, for Davidson was a hoodlum. A fixer of things, thug for hire for one James Hutchinson. Hutchinson was high up in the Inverness crime scene, very hard to touch, and a bit of a maverick, getting his fingers in many pies. But when things came crashing down, Davidson was the one who sent out the muscle to quieten things up. It was unusual for him to send someone like this.

'But you were sent to follow me. Is that correct? I don't think you're here to silence me because I don't meddle in Mr. Davidson's affairs.'

'Just follow you,' he said, 'find out who you were talking to.'

'Do you know who I am?' asked Dominic.

'No,' said the man. 'Given your photograph, told to find you. Was given your home address.'

Dominic didn't believe he had his home address, but Dominic did have a number of places he could operate out of, places that certain contacts believed he lived.

'Okay, so he sent you to follow me. Did he say why?'

'Mr. Davidson never says why. He just tells me what to do.' This was fair comment and Dominic was happy to let the man away with this one.

'I'm about to go about my business. I don't want to see you anywhere near me. I'm going to let you up now. You're going to walk out of the driveway. You're going to take a right and you're going to go back into town along the exact route that we came out on. Am I clear?' The man nodded. 'If you don't, I will see you and I will finish you.'

Dominic had no intention of finishing the man, but he wanted to scare him. Slowly, Dominic let off the tie around the man's throat and the man hauled himself up and turned to face Dominic.

'No, no, no. We don't look back at me. We just keep walking.' Dominic was afraid of one thing, that the man would want to show a bit of strength before leaving. He might want to land Dominic with one before disappearing. After all, the man had been made. He was useless now and Dominic would spot him a mile off. Not that he'd had difficulty spotting him in the first place.

Dominic watched the man closely, observing him with a trained eye, and that was why he saw the fist begin to move. There was a slight tweak of the hips, and then the man had turned around fully, throwing a right hook towards Dominic. Dominic stepped sideways, launched himself forward, placing one hand on the man's hip, driving his knee right up between his legs. The man doubled over as Dominic put a chop into the back of his neck.

'If there wasn't so much mess to clear up, I would finish you right now,' and Dominic put a kick into the man's stomach.

'Understand that. Don't let me see you again.'

The man rolled around on the ground. Dominic took his rucksack and calmly marched off along the road. There hadn't seemed to be anybody in the house, for which Dominic was glad. As he hurried off down the road before taking another left, heading back into town, he wondered why such heat was on. *Yes, they'd staked out the seller. Yes, they'd brought a lot of people in, but none of them were Hutchinson's men. Why was Hutchinson sending Davidson out, sending him to tail?*

One of the difficulties in this game was knowing who knew your cover and who didn't, and which cover. Dominic had worked the business a long time and now, at the age of fifty, he was thinking that maybe he should take a desk job. But he was too good at it and most of the time, he didn't have to resort to any violence. He was shrewd enough, quick enough, and wise enough not to get into any fight he couldn't get out of.

Back in town, Dominic crossed the bridge over the River Ness before making his way into an area that contained several pawnshops. He looked for the one that said McKenzie and opened the door, causing a little bell on top to announce his presence.

Inside, he thought he was in an antique shop, so old were most of the items around him. Most of the pawn shops had some modern equipment: computers, games, bikes, anything that could be sold on, but this was like an old classic shop—everything an antique. From the back of the shop, an old woman with white hair tied up in a bun at the back approached from behind the counter before setting her arms down on it, looking over at Dominic, and announcing, 'Can I help you?'

'Mrs. McKenzie,' said Dominic, 'I think you can.'

'I'm sorry, sir, I don't seem to know your name?'

'No, you don't.'

Then Dominic took a chance. 'I'm just looking for an update for Mr. Hutchinson.' The woman seemed to shiver, and she took a step back off the counter with her hands reaching down below it.

'No, no, there's no need for that. I'm just here for an update. It's not an ultimatum. It's not one of those calls, ma'am. It's just, a friendly enquiry.'

Dominic tried to pitch the words correctly, to sound threatening because anybody from Hutchinson would always sound threatening, but also to leave it open so that she wouldn't reach for the gun that was clearly beneath the counter. He watched her hands come back up onto the counter, but the sweat was still running down her face.

'I've been looking everywhere,' she said, 'I've put out feelers, we all have, but every time someone gets close, things happen.'

'What do you mean, things happen?'

'Well,' said the woman, 'we tried to reach the seller, the original seller, the European gentleman, but he's dead. They found him inside a bin lorry.'

Dominic put on a shocked face, but inside he was leaping for joy because he knew he was on the right lines. Coleen McKenzie may have looked like a little old lady, but throughout her life, she had trafficked, fenced, and moved on all sorts of items that the police wanted to know about. Intelligence had caught on to her some time ago, but it was deemed better to let her continue as she was a source of information, even if she didn't know it. In the past, other units had fed in and discovered from her important information about various goods, allowing them to go investigate and see who the real culprits were. Having acquired this information from his colleagues and other parts of the services, Dominic was now putting it to good use.

'I'm afraid Mr. Hutchinson is going to want better than that; he'd like to acquire the item.'

'Mr. Hutchinson might want to acquire the item, but I would respectfully say to him that the item is too hot to acquire. Other interested parties, parties that we don't know.'

'Parties from overseas?' asked Dominic.

'Several,' said the woman, 'and parties that are liable to take the item without prejudice. You can tell Mr. Hutchinson, he's going to need to have quite an armoury behind him to acquire said item. I can find it for him, but I'm in no position to actually acquire it.'

'Mr. Hutchinson will not be happy about that,' said Dominic, and then realised he'd overstepped the mark as the woman's hands went under the counter again.

'I think our meeting's at a close,' she said, and Dominic wondered how to play this. He shook his head and walked slowly up to the counter, his arms out wide so she knew he wouldn't be going for a gun. Reaching forward over the counter, he slapped the woman's cheeks with his hands in a friendly fashion before reaching forward and kissing her on the forehead.

'Mr. Hutchinson always rewards those that do well. That's why he sends me. Let's hope you see me next time and not the other bloke. Find it for him, Mrs. McKenzie; you hear me?' and with that Dominic walked towards the door, his ears straining in case she made for the gun. He doubted it; after all, it was broad daylight, and her shop was in an inhabited area. She'd have to have a silencer on it, which, in fairness, a woman like her could acquire, but Dominic reckoned she'd have the better sense to remain discreet.

As he stepped out of the door and onto the street, he felt a bead of sweat rolling down his face and he quickly mopped it off his brow. *Well, well,* thought Dominic, *that's interesting, too dangerous to touch even for a Hutchinson.*

Dominic spent the rest of the day moseying his way between different fences within Inverness. In each, he found either a person who didn't know what he was talking about or the same story as Mrs. McKenzie was giving. Wherever the diamond was, whatever it was, it was going to be a big deal. Around about teatime, he took a phone call from Justin, advising him that Kirsten would be back that night and she wanted to hold a conference back at the base. Seeing as it was five o'clock, he decided to return to one of his flats within the city and to grab a couple of hours of sleep. With what had gone on that day, Dominic reckoned this would be a long meeting.

Chapter 6

Kirsten traipsed up the stairs of their Inverness base, leaving behind the pretend front and lower office where a real business existed as cover. It was a funny thing within the service that there were people who knew nothing about what they did, but they were happy to accept what were effectively free premises and a modicum of risk, to create a facade that allowed the more nefarious works to be masked. However, at this time of the night, downstairs was closed and Kirsten walked through the dark until she reached the back stairs and made her way up to the higher floors.

She first made for her own office, finding it dark, and then switching on the light to see a note from Justin. It stated he'd arranged a meeting for eleven o'clock, and Kirsten glanced at her watch, seeing it was half an hour until that time. The man had clearly judged the flight times and travel correctly. The flight happened to have been interesting, as she'd climbed aboard an ambulance plane and had sat holding the hand of someone with no idea of who it was. The person looked to be in a bad way, and maybe he was, or maybe not. But when they landed in Inverness, she was discreetly whisked away while an ambulance took the man onward. Recovering her car, she had made her way back into town.

It was dark outside and the rain of the day had given way to a cold night. Kirsten looked down at some of the papers, a habit she'd got into, checking to see if any news was significant. Often the press got the first wind of things. There, at the bottom of the front page, was an article about the largest cruise ship in the world coming to the highlands. Hope had said something about that. Kirsten was just glad it was somebody else's business to take care of any protection around it. No doubt, certain factions could see it as a target and there would be noises made among the more restless natives. Still, it'd be nice to be holed up in one of those suites.

Of course, Kirsten's would have to be a proper suite, two floors, balcony on the outside, and somebody there, somebody there to share with. She slumped down in the seat behind her desk, elbow on the table, and put her chin in her hand. It hadn't been that long ago that she'd been delighted with this job. Delighted to be moved up, and in truth, she still enjoyed the job. It was still what she wanted to do, but she was starting to feel lonely because no one seemed to understand her anymore.

Her old friends, if she met them, couldn't be told what she was doing. Did she need someone in the know to confide in? But then again, that was the point of this job, wasn't it? You didn't confide, you held it all in. Secrets could be everything.

Kirsten shook her head, stood up, and made her way across the room to find her coffee machine had still not been cleared out. She had tried to get Justin to do it, baiting him that it was what should be done for the boss every day, but he wasn't biting. Although she did note when she was in the office, he came in and did it. A little shudder ran down her. She shook her head. The guy knew what he was doing. He was important to have around, even if he was a not-so-old old perv.

Kirsten emptied out the coffee and placed some more ground coffee into the filter before filling the machine up with water, pressing the button and allowing it to do its work. She walked over to the window, looked down in the street below, her eyes not focusing anywhere, her mind wandering. They might have to be quick on this, make a grab for it. And with London involved as well, things must be serious with it.

As a waft of fresh coffee hit her nose, she made a beeline back to the machine, poured herself some black liquid, and then took it through to the conference room, noting the time was ten minutes to eleven. As she opened the door, Justin Chivers put up a hand, saying hello, and then dove back down into his computer. He was clearly working on something he was going to present, which made Kirsten glad, because she was still wearing her outfit from the day.

Taking a seat, she sipped her coffee and thought back to the time just before the flight, when Johnson, the driver, had taken her for a coffee. They'd sat and talked about nothing in particular. Apparently, he liked windsurfing and Kirsten told him about being a mixed martial arts fighter in the ring. The time had flown, and soon after, he was dropping her off, but Kirsten found herself treasuring the moment. Just a chat with a stranger, just a momentary relaxing of the rules in life. She hadn't, of course, told him anything he could use, anything that wasn't generally known, and she was sure he hadn't either. However, it felt like the most intimate thing she'd done in the last two months. She was unsure whether to be sad about this or happy that it had happened.

The door opened and Dominic came in, giving a nod of his

head to the boss before sitting. Carrie-Anne followed shortly afterwards, closing the door behind her, while Justin turned down the lights.

'I gathered you all in,' said Kirsten, 'because I've been to London today. They're advising that we have a serious situation on our hands with these diamonds. We're after one diamond in particular. It's reasonably large, it has a slight green tinge to it, and it happens to hold a place in the hearts of some gentlemen in the Middle East. It's known in English as *The Light of the World*. Apparently, it's from their area but London is not telling me much more beyond that and I think that's because we need to deny we ever knew they were involved.'

'How do you mean?' asked Dominic.

'It's basically like this. The foreign power has had this gemstone taken, and I believe they threatened our government that if it doesn't come back, they're going to take action on our soil. Government officials clearly don't want any of this written in the papers and don't want to make a big show of it, so they're not telling even me what country this is from. All I've been told to do is hunt down this diamond, retrieve it, and I assume London will then hand it back to the correct country.'

'That sounds simple enough,' said Carrie-Anne. 'Grab it, get it sorted, then that's lovely.'

'If it was only so easy,' said Kirsten. 'Apparently, there's another Middle Eastern country that wants to embarrass them by taking it. They're involved at the moment.'

'And to complicate matters further,' said Dominic, 'James Hutchinson's after it.'

'Hutchinson?' said Kirsten, shocked. 'Something like this? He's not equipped to handle this.'

'I'm not sure he knows exactly what it is. There's obviously been noise about after what we heard of it,' said Dominic. 'And I think he's gone for it. You know what he's like. He's an opportunist. Put his hands on whatever pie. If it all gets messy, he'll send people there to clear it up.'

'That's not a good development,' said Justin. 'And I've more bad news for you, because he's not the only one interested.'

'How'd you mean?' asked Kirsten.

'Well, I was talking to some people in Interpol today when you were away, and I know for a fact the Swiss collector Kian Furrer is after it.'

'That's a new one on me,' said Kirsten. 'Who's Kian Furrer?'

'Kian Furrer has been around for a long while,' said Dominic. 'His name's come up when certain valuable items move about. He's a nasty sod with it. He's prepared to kill, or at least his people are. He doesn't tend to have his own. He has a small security detail, I believe, where he lives, but he hires out, which could be a problem for us.'

'He could put hitmen on the scene, is that what you're saying?' asked Kirsten.

'Most likely,' said Dominic. 'I've had scrapes before. He's a serious player.'

'So, we've got Mr. Furrer ready to kill and come and get it,' said Kirsten, 'we've got Hutchinson, who's going to storm in who knows what way because he hasn't got a clue what he's doing, and we've got a couple of Middle Eastern states ready to go at it. I don't know about you, but four of us seems rather light on this.'

'That's the play from London,' said Carrie-Anne. 'That's what they want. They want you in, grab it, get it over to the foreign state, and then that's it. The country's out of it. What they do after that, London won't care. As long as it's out of the UK, they can sit there and blow each other up, shoot each other dead and fight over it all they want, and to be frank,' the woman stretched her arms out, 'that's fine by me. I'm with London on this, but you didn't hear it from this Welsh girl.'

Kirsten smiled. 'I want to hear more about your research,' said Kirsten to Justin. 'I take it that you've got some stuff there.'

'I've got what we've got on him. I've got James Hutchinson as well, and I have no idea about any of these Middle Eastern states.'

'Good, because I don't either and I doubt Anna's going to tell me much.'

For the next hour, Justin flashed through details of Hutchinson's locale, his operators, much of which Kirsten knew already, but at a time like this, reminding themselves and bringing things again to the forefront of their mind was important. The next hour after that was taken up with Kian Furrer, and Kirsten made mental notes as she went along. The guy definitely seemed to be a piece of work. She noticed a shooting in Germany, barbaric in the extreme, all on the hunt for some emerald. When Justin had gone through his presentations, he turned to Kirsten.

'So, what next, boss? How'd you want to play this?'

'Well, how do we play it?' asked Kirsten. 'The Middle Eastern states, I mean, what do we do? Contact the local police force and say just detail us an all-Arab-men on the move? Of course not. They're not going to use people who look like they come from the Middle East, but that means they'll use players, people from here. Let's get on to our contacts. Carrie-Anne, Dominic, go back through your people, see what you can find—although I reckon they'll be keeping it very tight. Justin, I want you to get some taps on Hutchinson's men. Take some of your boys, set it up. You probably won't need to go that deep into the organisation. Some of the low-level guys will probably be hearing things. We just need a way in, if you understand me.'

Justin nodded, and Kirsten looked around her team. It was much simpler working on her own or working with somebody above giving the instructions, but now, she was the boss. Anna merely handed out the task; it was Kirsten's job to see it through. She was worried. This could get nasty very, very easily. A real cause for concern was Hutchinson. Who knew what he might do, how he might interrupt things?

Most searches for items like this, diamonds, artefacts, they were done very discreetly. The people who looked to acquire them didn't want to bring the attention of any local governments or even national governments. The Middle Eastern aspect, however, made this one especially important to keep quiet, but Hutchinson was known for being brutal, stomping in, finding things out, making a mess of it, and then sending in people to clear it up. Above all that, would Kian Furrer have somebody on the move? Somebody there, a hired gun to step in and sweep the gem away?

Kirsten wished the team good luck and dismissed them before standing up and making her way back into her office. She took off the jacket she'd been wearing all day, hung it up on the hook behind the door, collapsed into her chair, and took off the high-heeled shoes. The soles of her feet were sore, and she was glad she hadn't had to run at any point in them because they would've got kicked off straight away.

This was an awkward time, a time when she would have to wait for her team, see what they came back with. Kirsten thought she should really get some sleep, with the time now half past one. She could mosey down to the camp bed in one of the rear rooms and grab a couple of hours. But she knew she wasn't going to.

It was a mix of two things. The job was ongoing. She was excited for it, determined to get there, to find this gem, show everybody what she could do, and how her new team operated. But there was something else, and her mind drifted back to that coffee. *He'd been nice, hadn't he*, she thought. *He really had.*

Kirsten turned and locked her door. This was a precaution against Justin Chivers walking in. For now, she took off her blouse, changed her bra for a more supportive one, before pulling a t-shirt on over her top and then dropping her skirt to put on some Lycra shorts. From the corner of her room, she took a large bag and hung it from the ceiling hook in the middle. For twenty minutes, Kirsten kicked the living daylights out of it before punching it, attacking the bag with gusto. This was what she knew, this was her. Whenever things got tense, it was the best way to release, but she found herself stopping every now and again, her mind drifting back to that driver.

There came a knock at the door, and she turned to unlock it to find Justin Chivers.

'I thought you were killing someone,' he said.

'You're safe for the moment, Justin. I'm just working out, as usual. Was there anything important?' She looked into his face, stared at his eyes, daring him to keep his eyes on her face and not to look anywhere else.

'No, no. Just wanted to check you were okay.'

'Go,' she said. 'If you haven't got any of those taps set up by the morning, I'm going to come for you.'

He turned, put his hand up to the air, and said, 'Promises, promises.'

'You shouldn't speak to your boss like that,' she said, and

launched a gentle kick at his backside. The man hesitated before jumping forward.

Kirsten shut the door and began to think. *Why would he do that?* she thought. *Just turn up with no excuse. Just turn up as if to say I only arrived for a look. To let me know that. Before, yes, but not now I'm his boss*, she thought.

Something was bothering her about the whole Justin Chivers persona. He pulled the wool over everybody else's eyes, along with Anna Hunt. They had set up an entire belief amongst the service that the two of them didn't get on and he couldn't be trusted, that he leaked information. It was a masterstroke and done well. Now Kirsten thought she didn't really know him. Something about what he just did felt very uncomfortable and not just the fact that he was making out he was some sort of perv and dropping in on her. Surely no man would be that obvious.

You don't know men. That was the voice of an aunt, one from her past. *Yes, I do*, thought Kirsten, *and there's something up about him.*

Chapter 7

Justin Chivers walked from his desk to give the pot of tea a shake, pouring it out into a delicate China cup. He brought the cup back to his desk and sat down once more behind his computer. He was scanning through various recordings of phone taps that had been placed on Hutchinson's men. Of course, Justin didn't do the dirty work himself; he had a small team, none of whom were known to Kirsten, or indeed to anyone else, not even Anna Hunt, who had been given the addresses and the phone numbers, and would then make their way to setting up communications monitoring on whatever lines were required. However, due to circumstances, and sometimes the locations of these lines, taps or line monitoring were not always completely accurate, and a certain amount of distortion would often come in. On the current recording, Justin was having trouble trying to clean it up.

It was a call from what Justin would have described as a middleman. Someone not very high ranking in the organisation, but who was tasked with pulling certain people together, muscle, in general, if it was required for an evening. Hutchinson and his senior men were much better at covering up what they were doing, but these lower ranks, having not had much information, were often passing calls over open landlines or through their mobiles.

There was a rap at his office door. Justin looked up to see Dominic at the window, asking if it was okay to come in. He was doing so because of the large earphones on Justin's head, but he took them off, having not started the next recording, and waved Dominic through.

'Any luck yet?'

'There's possibly something in this recording. I'm trying to clean it up at the moment,' said Justin. 'What about you?'

Dominic walked over to the coat rack in Justin's office and took off a smart overcoat he'd been wearing. Underneath, he was dressed in a shirt and a tie with suit trousers on. Clearly, he'd been paying calls on people of class—either that or he was trying to give off a certain persona.

'No, nothing so far. At least nothing that we don't know already. Everyone is very quiet right now.'

'Not this guy. There's tea in the pot if you want it, Dom. I'm going to put the bins back on. Have another listen.'

Justin put his headphones on again, pressed play on the recording and listened intently, but his eyes watched Dom making his way across where he swirled the teapot. Pouring the liquid into a mug, which Dominic had brought in himself, instead of one of the China cups, made Justin give a shake of the head. You couldn't install class into some people.

He was still intently listening as Dom made his way back and sat down in the chair in front of Justin's desk. Dom gave the impression that he was simply killing time and had no cares in the world at all. Justin wondered if that was when Dom was doing his major thinking. Then a word passed his ear. Addison. Addison F. What on earth was Addison F? He let the recording run for another twenty seconds, but the distortion was hard to eliminate. Tonight. One more word. Tonight.

Justin took the bins off his ears, placed them down, and looked over his laptop at Dom on the other side. 'There's something going on tonight. Some sort of meet they're taking muscle to. Addison. Addison F.'

'Why don't you Google it? Put it on the map, see what comes up?'

'You think I'm not doing that?' said Justin, almost annoyed by the comment. Justin had his head down now, watching the screen, tapping away on his keyboard like he was trying to save the Earth. 'There's nothing. There's no Addison F. No Addison Farm. No Addison fare, No Addison whatever. I can't find anything.'

'Easy,' said Dom, 'maybe that's not what they mean. Maybe Addison's a person.'

'Maybe,' said Justin, 'do you know anybody called Addison?'

'Scam the records,' said Dom and came round the desk to look at Justin's screen. This time Justin didn't rush, instead, taking his China teacup between his thumb and forefinger, while sipping gently on the tea inside.

'What's that muck in there anyway?' asked Dom.

'Lady Grey, it's got that little orange zesty feel, doesn't it? A little bit more delicate than Earl Grey, I find.'

Justin could see Dom wasn't impressed, and instead just stared at the screen waiting for Justin to get on with it. 'Okay, okay. Here we go.'

Justin began tapping into various databases of known criminals, searching up Addison. It wasn't long before he found a Luke Addison. He was a bouncer at an establishment in Inverness known as a gentleman's club.

'Shall I go and check this one out?' said Justin. Dom rolled his eyes.

'I'm on it. Don't worry. I'll be back within the hour. Give Kirsten a ring. Let her know what I've come up with.'

'What you've come up with? I think I did the spadework.'

'I'll let you take that one,' said Dom. 'The spadework. Yes, you did the spadework. I was merely the genius.' He stood up, grabbed his overcoat, and made his way out of the office.

'Bloody cheek,' said Justin. Lifting his cup against his lips, he chewed over his tea as he swirled it round his mouth. Having enjoyed the beverage, he placed the cup down, picked up his phone, and rang Kirsten.

***

It was a cold day in Inverness, but last night's rain was gone and the time was approximately six o'clock. One thing that always astonished Dom about gentlemen club establishments was the fact that many of them could be open right through the day. Did these people who went along not work? Now, Dom was no prude. He was as red-blooded as the next man as he would have put it but he was very uneasy about what went on, about which of the women were actually there by choice. Or at least there because they needed the money. He knew that many of the clubs operated above board, but there were a number that he certainly was not sure about.

This particular one was owned by James Hutchinson, although he would never be seen inside. Dom didn't care about that. He was waiting for Luke Addison with a photograph of the man inside his coat. Unlike when he'd been tailed previously, and he'd taken on the larger six feet four monster, as some people would've put it, Dominic was feeling much more uneasy about tackling this suspect. The man was reportedly handy in a fight. When you're five feet six and people are talking about you being handy in a fight, you can usually take care of yourself.

Dominic thought about going inside, wondering if the man would disappear out of a rear entrance, but instead, he waited at the front, scanning the street as he sat in his car. He'd had to push the warden on several times, flashing a badge that she recognised so she would ask no questions. It was just after nine o'clock when he finally saw Luke Addison emerging from the club. The man was short with blond hair that had been smoothed over to one side. He had a leather jacket on, along with dark jeans and a shirt underneath. Dominic couldn't see clearly, but he swore there must be a medallion under there somewhere. On Luke's arm was a tall girl.

Girl, was that the right word? thought Dom. *Surely, she was a woman. She was clearly working in the club, so she must have been a woman, but no, she looked like a girl. Maybe she was new, but she certainly was arm-in-arm with Addison.*

He watched the pair of them walk along the road, and then stand at the bus stop. Exiting his car, he followed along, standing a couple of feet from them, looking elsewhere, and occasionally bringing out a paper he had in his pocket to read. When the bus came along and he saw them move for it, Dominic followed and was grateful when they made their way, all the way to the rear, taking up a seat just in front of the back row. Dominic followed and sat down behind them, but he could see that Luke Addison was suddenly becoming suspicious. Carefully, Dominic put two fingers together from one hand and prodded them into Addison's back.

'Don't move, or I will fire. It'll be slow as well. I'm not firing down at your heart and I'm not firing at your head, but I guess it might take a piece of neck off. Certainly leave you a big wound.' The girl spun round looking into Dominic's face, and he glared at her. 'Eyes front, lady.'

She spun back. 'You turn again, and I'll shoot you.' Dom could see her beginning to shake.

'Okay. This is what's going to happen. What's your name, love?'

The girl looked in front and whispered, 'Debbie.'

'Okay, Debbie,' said Dom, 'ring the bell, the button, the red one. Next stop, get off. Go home and get a proper job.'

'I'm an artist,' said the girl, suddenly affronted.

'They gave up that sort of art in the eighteenth century. Just ring the bell and get off. I need a word with Mr. Addison.'

Dominic could see the man shiver a little when he realised that Dom knew his name. The bus slowed down as the girl rang the bell, and she got off at the next stop. As she made her way off the bus, Dominic could understand why Addison was trying to take her home.

'A bit strange taking a girl like that, when you've got a meeting tonight.'

'Who said I had a meeting?'

Dom pressed his fingers harder into the back of Addison. 'Got a knife here as well. Quite happy to start nicking bits of ear off. It's all right, I can see the CCTV screen, and frankly, I don't care. I've been sent by some gentlemen. They want to know where the meeting is.'

Addison shuddered, but Dom wasn't fully convinced. 'What sort of people?' asked Addison.

'The kind who don't take no for an answer. Well, at least the kind that shoot you if you say no.'

'Okay,' said Addison. 'If it's going to be like that, Strathpeffer is where you want to go. Strathpeffer tonight, eleven o'clock.'

'Whereabouts in Strathpeffer?'

'There's a load of shops, a museum and that, inside a train station, down from the main bit on the way out of Strathpeffer. Cuts into the back. They're taking over one of those shops in there tonight. It'll be dark apart from it, probably.'

'What was your role in all this?'

'What my role always is, stand there and hit anybody that he tells me to.'

'Who tells you to?'

'The boss.'

'And the boss is?'

'It's Klingon.'

Dominic shook his head. *What did the man mean, Klingon?* 'Who the heck's Klingon?'

'Vicious so he is. Likes his violence. We call him Klingon.'

'What do you call him, when you need to tell the government about him?'

'Paul Mathers.'

'Is Mr. Mathers going to be there tonight?'

'How should I know? I'm just going. Can I get off now?'

Dom was getting the feeling that Luke was not feeling particularly threatened.

'Aren't you bothered that they're going to get you for giving up the details?'

'Well, you're not going to tell them, are you?' said Addison, 'and I don't intend to tell them either.'

'Make sure you don't, or you and your little lady will come to a nasty end. Now, ding the bell, and get off at the next stop.'

Dom watched the man press the red button, and the bell sounded on the bus. It pulled over shortly and Luke Addison exited.

Dom got off at the next stop, realised he was on the other side of Inverness, and started to walk back towards where he'd parked his car. He made a circuitous route rather than walk straight to the street it was in, looking all the time to see if he was being followed but when he realised he wasn't, he got into the car and drove off. Time was against him. He needed to get the team moving, so he picked up the phone and gave Kirsten a call.

'I think I've got it,' he said. 'The place where they're meeting tonight.'

'Is it definitely it?'

'I think so.'

'How do you know?' asked Kirsten.

'They gave me it too easy. It's almost like they wanted us to be there.'

'How do you mean?' asked Kirsten.

'Just a feeling,' said Dom. 'Just a feeling we were meant to find out.'

Chapter 8

Kirsten closed off the call and immediately ran out of her office and into Justin Chivers. 'Whatever you're doing, put it down. We need to get on the move. Grab some of your listening equipment.'

'Why?' asked Justin.

'We're going to Strathpeffer,' said Kirsten. 'Dom's found out where it is—he said eleven o'clock. The time now is ten; we need to shift.'

'Okay,' said Justin. 'It will take me ten minutes to get everything together.'

'You've got five,' said Kirsten. 'I said we need to shift,' and with that, she was out the door. She was feeling more herself now dressed in black jeans, black T-shirt, and a leather jacket, her hair tied up behind her and stout black boots on her feet. Kirsten shouted into Carrie, who was sleeping in the makeshift restroom. 'We need to go in five minutes, Carrie. Dark attire. We're on op.'

'Bloody hell,' said Carrie, rolling the covers away. 'You're worse than my last boss, do you realise that?'

Kirsten laughed as she left the room, but inside, she could feel the excitement building. It was ten minutes before Justin

Chivers arranged all his gear in the van and they drove off from the back alley of the house out into the Inverness night. Strathpeffer involved routing north towards Dingwall and then cutting off into the village. Kirsten knew it reasonably well, being home to the Highland Museum of Childhood and the Strathpeffer Pump Room, and she believed she'd actually been to the location Dom had described.

It had the look of an old railway station, but there was a neat road to the building at the bottom of Strathpeffer and now it was a museum. There was a covered archway on the far side from the car park and several ways you could walk in, but there wasn't any quick way out. As Kirsten remembered it, there was only one way in, but there was a road at the far end. She tried to drag out of her head what it looked like considering she was now going there in the dark, but she couldn't bring it to mind.

They picked Dom up on the way to Inverness and he began to change in the back of the van. Soon everyone except Justin was in black.

'How do we want to play this,' asked Justin, driving the van.

'It looks like we're going to come late to the party, so we'll close in, try and approach through other houses.' She looked at the map in front of her provided by the internet. 'There,' she said and pointed to a road before the turning to the Highland Museum of Childhood. 'We can turn in there,' said Kirsten, 'route through the back of the Ben Wyvis Hotel, take the path down, and come in from that side. You can give us some of your devices, Justin, to try to listen to what's going on. We'll see if we can spread out. I'll try and get Dom in close. We need to either close the place down or we need to recover the stones, but until we see the gems, we don't do anything, okay?'

'I've still got this feeling,' said Dom, 'that they want us here.'

'Why do you think?' asked Kirsten.

She saw Carrie-Anne with her face looking towards the van roof and she could understand that she was thinking aloud.

'Well,' said Carrie-Anne to no one, 'if we're there and other people can have their attention on us, maybe he's thinking he could take the stones.'

'Hutchinson isn't actually invited to this?'

'That'll be my take. Otherwise, why bring us?' offered Carrie-Anne. 'If he was invited genuinely, if he was going to bid for it, fair enough, but if he's not invited, let's bring the law in as much as we are. He can divert things onto us and he might have somebody there to grab stuff and go.'

'Let's clock the faces when we get down and see if any of them look like Hutchinson's men, okay?' said Kirsten.

It was approximately ten past eleven when they parked up and ran through the rear of the Ben Wyvis Hotel, before making their way down to sit in the trees across from the Highland Museum of Childhood. Kirsten could see the covered walkway and a number of figures walking up and down. One solitary room was lit up and through the window, Kirsten could see some anxious people waiting.

'Delta,' whispered Kirsten through her comms, 'do you recognise anyone here?'

'Negative,' replied Dom.

'You said your man was coming tonight, didn't you? Can you see him?'

'Negative,' said Dom. 'He said he was going to be on the walkway.'

'Carrie-Anne,' said Kirsten, 'fan out wider and see who's on the perimeter.'

There was a double-tap on the microphone and Kirsten didn't even see her move off into the dark. Kirsten's hand went inside her jacket checking her weapon was there again with the silencer on.

Kirsten waited in the dark looking either way and continued to see the men patrolling up and down the covered walkway. The white iron that supported the walkway's roof glistened wet in the light as a soft drizzle of rain began to fall.

'This is Charlie. Found Delta's man. He's just arrived, but he's not coming inside. He's across the road. A few of them are joining up. They seem to be carrying a lot of torches.'

Kirsten didn't feel comfortable. 'Delta,' she said to Dom, 'move in closer. See if you can find any items of interest.'

There was a double-tap again on the microphone and Kirsten took out her binoculars looking at the room with the light. One man had his back to her and was clearly talking to someone in front of him. Kirsten was desperate to know who this was because it was a potential buyer. However, she bided her time and looked for an update from Carrie-Anne.

'Charlie here. Hutchinson's men, as I think, are making their way to the Museum. They're walking down the road, but I think one of the guns on the platform is starting to notice them.'

'Keep an eye, ' said Kirsten. 'Let me know if they come closer.'

'Delta here. Can you see who's in that room?'

'Negative,' said Kirsten. 'Have you got an angle?'

'Affirm. The man inside looks Middle-Eastern.'

At that moment, the man in the room who was covering the view moved away and Kirsten got to look at the figure Dom was referring to. He certainly looked like he was from the Middle East, but London had said they wouldn't come themselves.

'Eyes on, Delta,' she said. 'Don't let that man leave. The goods may be going with him.'

'Charlie here. A car just arriving.'

'Who is it?' asked Kirsten.

'Tall, wearing sunglasses, blond, European looking. Don't know them.'

Kirsten wondered what was going on, but soon, she saw the blond man step onto the platform where he was frisked down by a couple of guards. Then he put his gun to one side on the floor before he proceeded along with his bag to enter the room where the Middle Eastern man was located.

'Got to get closer, Delta. Got to get closer.' Kirsten looked over the edge and could see Dom. It'd be awkward for him to move along the walkway without being seen. She watched as he disappeared behind the building possibly looking to come up from the other side. It was another three minutes before she heard, 'Delta in position.' Kirsten scanned left and right along the platform, but there was nothing, and then she looked up seeing Dom on the roof. He was using a small drill picking a tiny hole in the roof which he looked down into.

'What you got, Delta?'

'There's a bag on the table. He's opened it. A lot of diamonds. I can't tell from here if the important one is there.'

'Get ready to move,' said Kirsten. 'Charlie, bring yourself back around to support.'

Suddenly, several large bright torches shone at Kirsten's face. As luck would have it, she was in the trees, but she was not that far back. Kirsten realised straight away she'd be lit up like a Christmas tree, obvious to all the guards in the platform. She saw the weapons begin to be lifted and ran off into further coverage as gunshots came towards her.

'Delta, they're packing up.'

'Secure that package, Delta,' said Kirsten, breathless as she heard men begin to enter the trees behind her. She cut left behind a larger tree and heard the shots disappear over her right shoulder. She circled around, peered into the dark, and saw a man coming towards her. He had a large gun in front of him and Kirsten dispatched him straight away, barely a retort coming from her gun with the silencer on the end. The man following him turned and ran to find cover and Kirsten made her way back towards the initial spot she had been in. The torchlight was now gone, but there seemed to be a lot more people on the scene.

'Charlie, where did they go, Hutchinson's men?'

'Charlie here. I think they broke cover. Could be them that lit you up.'

'Well, thanks for the heads up,' said Kirsten, angrily. She looked up across the walkway to see a door open from the room that the Middle Eastern man was in. He was now stepping outside with a bag, and the European man looking to disappear with a briefcase. Dom swung down from above, clattering into the Middle Eastern man. Kirsten saw the European draw his weapon and quickly fired off a shot that sent him plummeting back against the building before he fell forward.

'Delta, get down.' Kirsten watched Dom roll off the platform falling into the black of the ground in front of it. She saw someone coming towards him and fired her weapon again. Suddenly, she heard machine gunfire from the far end of the platform.

Dom was keeping himself well hidden, down below, but no

one was on the platform now except for one man. He ran forward to pick up the jewels. Kirsten circled around through the wood and saw the man with the machine gun at the end. She stepped up behind him, put an arm around, and twisted his neck before letting him fall to the ground.

Another man appeared from the rear of the buildings, but she dispatched him instantly before continuing to run around that side. A car was beginning to move and Kirsten shot the tyres out, but that did little damage compared to another car that ploughed into it. In the melee, Kirsten was unsure who was who. She ran through the walkway in the middle of the building, put her head around the corner to see the Middle Eastern man getting knocked to one side, the bag falling over and diamonds rolling this way and that.

'Delta, start rounding them up. We need to get them.'

A diamond rolled towards her. Kirsten swept down, taking it in her hand just as a man came around the corner at her. She didn't have time to fire but instead swung her leg out tripping the man up. He stumbled forward, smacked his head off the side of the building, and then received another punch to his head when he turned around.

'Charlie, where are you, Charlie?' asked Kirsten.

'Coming in from the street entrance. Just tagged two. These are all different people. It's chaos out here.'

'Agreed. Juliet, get word to the authorities. We need bigger backup here.'

'Requesting armed response. Juliet out.'

Kirsten's heart pounded. This had all gone crazily wrong, well, at least for her. She now believed that Hutchinson had played for this, but how many parties were involved?

Kirsten wondered how she was going to close this down,

finish it off. There was the public to think of as well if this crowd just vanished into the side streets of Strathpeffer. 'Charlie, hold the road entrance, nothing in, nothing out,' she said. 'Delta, get these diamonds. They're still all over the floor.'

'Trying,' came the response.

Kirsten stepped out onto the walkway, looked down to the far end, saw a gun being pointed, and moved herself back inside the walkway that went through the building. Leaning out, she fired off a couple of shots, spun back, and they ran up the wrong side of the house. In the car park, she saw several lights come on and started shooting at car lights, but it was chaos and she ducked down behind some recycling bins as gunfire ripped across. Kirsten saw some cars make for the exit.

'Charlie, are you there? The car is making for the exit, stop them. Extreme prejudice.'

There was no reply. Kirsten checked her mic. 'Charlie, respond. Charlie, respond.' Again nothing. 'Juliet, respond. Can you hear me?'

'Loud and clear.'

'Charlie, respond.'

Kirsten made her way out from behind the bins she was using for cover. She saw one man coming towards her and instantly shot him in the shoulder. She then ran avoiding a car, its wheels spinning in the mud, and got to the entrance where a number of cars had crashed on the road outside.

Kirsten ran up to the car that was leaving and put a gun up to the window, firing up into the roof. The window shattered, but from the front seat, another gun appeared. She threw herself to the ground. The car spun off, but as it did so, the streetlight cast its beam into the back of the vehicle.

She could see Carrie-Anne's face, a hand clamped over her mouth, a gun to her head.

'Charlie captured,' Kirsten screamed, 'Charlie captured. Juliet, where the hell's my backup?'

Chapter 9

Kirsten felt the blood pumping through her veins. She'd just seen her colleague taken away in a car and all sorts of thoughts were running through her head. *Would they simply execute her? Would they hold her for ransom? What was the purpose of having her?* Meanwhile, the scramble for the diamonds back on the platform at the childhood museum was still in full swing.

'Kilo, the items are still here. It's like a standoff. Most of them are just lying on the platform floor.'

'Delta, this is Kilo. They have Charlie. They have Charlie taken away. We need to move quickly.'

'This is Juliet. Do I pursue? If so, give description.'

Kirsten's mind boggled. She needed to get the job done here. London expected her to recover the *Light of the World* and to find out what was going on. There could be national implications at stake, but she had seen one of her own colleagues disappear. With the clock ticking, the woman's life could be in danger.

'Juliet, black Astra. Last three numbers of registration, four-six-niner. I say again, four-six-niner. Go.'

'Juliet, copy.'

'Delta, keep them off that platform any way you can. I'm coming to assist.'

'Roger.'

Kirsten could hear gunfire. Pretty soon this situation was going to get completely out of hand. She expected a simple trade-off, and although she put a covering call in for the police firearms team, this was meant to be a stake-out simply watching what happened, not sweeping in for a swift intercept. At least the firearms unit would be prepped and should already be on its way.

Kirsten made her way back from the entrance of the childhood museum towards the platform. As she did so, a car drove at her, lights flashing. She threw herself to one side. Many of the men had cut and run, so maybe some of the good diamonds had been taken. She made her way onto the platform, poking her head around the corner and saw someone at the far-end. Kirsten aimed her weapon, firing twice down the long-range. She didn't think she'd hit anyone, but whoever it was turned and moved away. She saw an opportunity for Dom to grab some of the diamonds that were up on top.

'Delta, platform clear. Go.'

From the side of the platform, she saw Dom throw himself up onto the platform and reach out for some diamonds. As he put his hand down, a man stepped out of one of the buildings, gave Dom a kick in the stomach, and then reached down. Kirsten aimed her weapon again and fired, tagging the man on his shoulder, but he seemed impervious.

Kirsten wondered if it was some sort of body armour he was wearing. One thing he did was to be quick, reaching down amongst the diamonds for a certain one, pocketing it, and then stepping back inside the building. Kirsten ran out onto the platform and when she saw someone put their head around the corner at the far end, she fired quickly.

'Delta, Delta, are you injured?'

She heard Dom spit, but he rolled himself sideways falling off the platform back into the black below. Kirsten ignored him, took a left to the door that the man who picked up the diamond had gone through. Seeing it wasn't open, she kicked it hard, sending it flying back into the room. Carefully, she looked around the corner of the door then entered, again, sweeping around, checking every corner, but the rear window was open.

She moved to the window, but before she could poke her head out, the glass exploded, and she threw herself backwards. Several shots peppered the window. Kirsten made her way back to the front door, ran along the platform and through the alcove that split the buildings. As she came out, she saw a car beginning to drive away and she fired at the wheels. A window was rolled down and she had to take cover as shots were fired back.

'Delta, where are you?'

'On my feet. Where do you need me?' said Dom, wheezing.

'In the car park. They're getting away.'

'I'll pick up a car. Keep your eyes on.'

Kirsten began to run after the vehicle that was disappearing ahead of her. From the side, she saw a man come from the trees. She aimed her gun and fired at him sending him tumbling back into the undergrowth, but the car ahead was picking up pace and leaving via the exit. Kirsten began to sprint for all she was worth, her eyes trained on the number plate. As the car spun out onto the road, another car clipped the back of it. Kirsten had to run around the rear to avoid getting hit by the car.

The car she was chasing momentarily slowed down, but then picked up pace again and started to pull away from her. Kirsten lifted her knees, put her head down, and concentrated on pumping her arms. She could hear no car coming behind her, none she could acquire to help her in the chase. She could ask Dom where he was with getting a car to assist, but it would only take the breath out of her, and she needed every bit she could get. She watched the rear lights of the car disappearing ahead of her as it left Strathpeffer heading down into a wooded road.

As her legs started to give out from underneath her, she heard a car behind her and flicked her head around but struggled to see who it was with the car headlights. She ran to one side crouching down her weapon at the ready. The car pulled up; the window went down.

'Get in,' said Dom. Kirsten stood up, opened the door, and closed it as Dom was already pulling away.

'Can you see the red light?' she said breathlessly.

'Just about.'

'Well, keep on it,' said Kirsten. 'I need to make a call.' She reached inside her black cargo trousers, pulled out her phone, and dialled the Inverness police station. She was put through to the tactical firearms unit who were already mobile. Kirsten detailed the situation at the platform, advised that most of the fugitives had run but the firearms crew were to proceed with caution, clear up as best they could. When asked where she was, Kirsten simply said she was in pursuit and closed the phone down.

'Juliet, status?' asked Kirsten.

Justin Chivers' voice came back rather agitated through her earpiece. 'They've headed down an estate. I think I've got them cornered. I'm not sure though. Had to break off pursuit because there's a number of people there.'

'What do you mean you had to break off pursuit?'

'There's people here armed at a gate. I'm in a large van and I can't handle a weapon very well. I had to break off pursuit.'

'Is Carrie in there?'

'It's a farm and I clocked the car. The car took her in.'

'Okay, hold your position at distance. Make sure nobody else comes out.'

'Kirsten,' said Dom, 'I'm not too sure I'm going to keep up with this pursuit. He's turning off into a housing estate there. We're going to struggle.'

Kirsten grabbed a piece of paper from inside her cargo trousers, and with a pencil, she wrote down the number plate of the car they were pursuing. She left it on the dash in front of Dominic. 'If we lose them, that's the number plate. Get onto the police. Get everyone looking for it.'

Dominic swore as he spun into the estate. The lights of the car were already gone. Dominic went round the estate seven or eight times, but the vehicle was nowhere in sight. *Had they doubled back and gone back onto the road? Had they taken one of the other smaller side roads? Had they parked up in a garage? Who knew?* Kirsten thought that the man she had seen pick up that particular diamond was the key to what London wanted. There were diamonds everywhere but he had been very specific.

Kirsten turned to Dominic, shaking her head. 'He's gone, Dom. Let's head back. Let's rendezvous with Justin, work out what we're going to do. They have Carrie.' The tension in Kirsten's voice was palatable, and she wondered what she was going to do. London had made it quite clear the objective was the diamond that had just gone missing. If she wasn't quick and acted on it, the lead would go cold and she'd have no idea where to go after the main prize.

The drive back to find Justin Chivers seemed to take an age and was completed in silence. Kirsten knew Dom was as apprehensive as she was about Carrie-Anne, but the man was a professional and he seemed to be an island of calm in the car. Kirsten, on the other hand, could feel her feet starting to tap. She was getting agitated.

They met up with Justin Chivers at the roadside in a small parking area. The time was now two in the morning, and the light drizzle that was present before had now increased to steady rain.

'She's over there,' said Justin, pointing to a farmhouse in the middle of a field. Kirsten looked and saw there was one road in and no others out.

'I take it that's it,' she said to Justin. 'They're protecting that one road, aren't they?'

'Very much,' he said. 'They didn't clock me, I drove past, but I clocked them. If you put your night vision on, you'll see them.' Kirsten picked up her binoculars with night vision capabilities, and could see a couple of figures along the roadside leading down to the farmhouse.

'How many have you counted so far?' she asked Justin.

'I've seen five outside,' he said. 'I doubt there'll be many more inside.'

'Dominic, I'm going to need someone to liaise with police, get after the diamond that's gone missing. You've got the car registration. The man who took it looked Middle-Eastern, which surprised me because I didn't think they'd be here.'

'Shouldn't you take that?' asked Dom. 'I mean, you're the

boss.'

'You're capable of handling it. I'm going to get Carrie-Anne. Take Justin with you.'

'Are you sure?' asked Dom. 'I can come in with you, give you backup.'

'I'm sure,' said Kirsten. 'They won't see me coming. What I do want is Justin here to put a call in to the police, direct them to this farmhouse in about two hours' time.'

'Won't that look a little bit suspicious with a load of dead bodies left over?'

'I'm not intending to kill anyone, Justin,' said Kirsten, 'but they'll need cleaned up.'

Dom turned and extended a hand to Kirsten, shaking hers. 'Go get her,' said Dom. 'I've got this.'

'If Anna calls, tell her I'm recovering our asset, but I'll be dark for the next hour or two.'

'She's going to be pretty pissed that your diamond went north,' said Justin.

Kirsten looked up at him. 'What else have we got in the back of the van?' she said. Together with Justin, she stepped in and sorted out her ammunition making sure she was fully loaded. She also made sure she had night goggles with her.

'Your top's ripped at the back,' said Justin. 'Have you noticed?' She allowed his hand to touch her skin as he poked his hand through up her shoulder.

'I hadn't,' she said. They looked around the inside of the van before pulling out one of the lockers and grabbing a t-shirt from within. She took off her jacket and hauled the top she had on off, although Justin was behind her. She reckoned she could feel him leer at her, but she ignored it and put her t-shirt on, tucked it into the cargo top, and grabbed another jacket.

'You could come rescue me anytime, do you realise that?' said Justin.

Kirsten turned around, looked him in the face, 'Not the time, Justin. Not really the time, but if I did, I'd come and put you down proper.' She brushed past him knocking the man to one side.

'Ooh, feisty. This is going to be good,' said Justin.

There was something in his comment that didn't ring true for Kirsten. The more she worked with Justin, the more she started to wonder how many layers there were to the man.

'You two better get going,' she said to Dom, and zipped up her jacket. 'I'll head off that way, come in from the far side.'

'Good plan,' said Dom. 'Give us a call when you're done. I'll be standing by in case you need medical backup.'

'Let's hope not,' said Kirsten. With that, she disappeared off into the dark of the night.

Chapter 10

'In an operative's life,' they had told her, 'there will come moments when you will be on your own up against it and feel the terror wash at you like a wave.' This was one of those moments. Kirsten fought to control the adrenaline rising inside her. She didn't know what she was going to see. Would she find Carrie-Anne in a room somewhere, beaten to a pulp? Worse, would her throat be slit? Would Kirsten find herself captured as well? There was always the fear, as a woman, that they wouldn't simply beat you up. Kirsten was well-used to that in the martial arts ring, but maybe in this situation they would use your body as well.

Kirsten sniffed. Well, the one thing they wouldn't do was take her alive, and if they'd used Carrie-Anne in any way like that, she'd bury them. Kirsten looked up at the farmhouse in the distance. She'd given herself half a mile to circling the farm. She was now approaching from the rear of the building.

Kirsten placed herself down flat in a ploughed field, but close into a hedge that ran along the edge. It would be a crawl of some three hundred metres, but Kirsten settled into it, slowly moving her arms forward and letting her knees follow, as gradually she picked her way across the muddy field beneath her. Her face was already blacked up from the previous operation, and she tried hard not to think of the possibilities ahead in terms of what had happened to Carrie-Anne, but rather, of the numbers she would face, and how to do this. The one thing she would have to be was quiet. With that in mind, she was intending not to use her gun unless she had to, even though it was silenced.

As she got close to the edge of the field, she thought she could hear, through the wind and the rain, someone on the other side. She froze, letting her ears pick up the sounds of the night. Sure enough, she could hear footsteps. Carefully, she rose, first to her knees, and then onto her feet, but keeping crouched. The hedge in front of her was thick, and she walked along, trying to find a thinner patch to move through. It was when she found it that she saw the feet that were making the noise on the other side.

Back and forward walked a man who was quite tall, well over six feet. This annoyed Kirsten, because she was small, and getting up to tackle a man of that size was not easy. She watched him walk past one way, then when he turned and came back the other way, she started to make her way slowly through the hedge. When she was on the far side, she congratulated herself for making no tell-tale signs, no twigs snapping, no crunch of the feet. The man up ahead was getting to the point in his route where he had previously made his turn to retrace his steps. Kirsten was now on his side of the hedge, and if he turned around, he would see her.

She ran quickly up behind him, making little noise. She jumped up, throwing one arm around his neck, her hand clamping over his mouth and a knee driving into his back. The man tumbled forward, and Kirsten landed on top of him, moving her knee deeper into his back, keeping it there, while her arm closed around tightly on his throat. It was a move she understood well. As she controlled him for the next thirty seconds, she waited for him to pass out. Having checked he'd gone limp and was indeed out for the count, she made her move towards the rear of the farmhouse.

There were lights on inside. Kirsten made her way up to the rear of the building, shuffling along the wall, listening in where she could. She had a fear for Carrie-Anne, because the woman had looks, a bubbly personality and gorgeously buoyant, blonde hair. She wasn't some plain figure that men wouldn't be interested in and all it took was one bad egg in the bunch of professionals, to turn it in from a bad situation to a thoroughly nasty one. Kirsten reached the rear farmhouse door and pushed open a small letterbox to see inside the hall.

There was no one there and she tried the handle, delicately lifting it, opening the door slowly in case it would squeak, before putting it back on its latch. Now inside, she was exposed, the lights on. She stepped forward, realising she was leaving muddy footprints behind her. However, there was no mat, no easy way to clean her trace.

At the front of the small corridor she was in, there was a set of stairs heading upwards. There was a door on the right, and another one she believed led to the kitchen on her left. She listened closely at the kitchen door but heard nothing. She checked the door on her right but, again, heard nothing inside, so slowly, she made her way to the front, crouching down because of the glass in the window at the front door. Taking the edge of the stairs, she climbed them. But from upstairs, she could hear something. There was a muffled cry and then the ripping of fabric.

Kirsten edged her way slowly to reach the landing at the top and realised she could only go left or right. There were two rooms up there. Both had the doors closed. She listened to the one on her right and could hear snores. Meanwhile, on her left, she heard what sounded like whimpering.

'You thought he'd protect you, didn't you?' said a man. 'But he's off for a sleep. I think it's time to have a little bit of fun.' Kirsten tensed up, and then heard what sounded like a slap across the face. Not something gentle, but something wild and vicious. Every instinct in her wanted to kick that door open, charge in, and tear into the man inside. She imagined Carrie-Anne being there in some uncompromising position, being manhandled by this fiend, but if she got this wrong, and he saw her and was able to get a cry off or a shout, they would be in serious trouble, the men out in the driveway coming in with guns. There was probably a radio link between them all, certainly if they were any type of professional.

Kirsten reached up to the door handle, ready to open it gently and look inside. She heard another slap and then there was more ripping of clothing.

'Oh, yes. Oh, you are splendid,' said a voice. Kirsten turned the handle of the door and very slowly edged it open. She could see a bare leg, recognised it to be a female one, presumably Carrie-Anne's. As she continued to open the door, she saw a leg beside it dressed in trousers. Slowly, she opened the door fully. Kirsten pushed from her mind the fact that her colleague did not seem to be wearing much. Carrie-Anne was tied to a chair, her face a mess from being slapped. Who knew if he'd beaten her up beforehand?

Carrie-Anne could see Kirsten in the background, but she was a professional, didn't stare, but simply looked up into the man's face, almost taunting him, despite the gag that was in her mouth. The man leant forward, his hands reaching out to her body and Kirsten crept behind him. She put an arm around him, pulling his neck back, her other hand going across his face. Once again, she applied the pressure, felt the man kicking, struggling, but this man was smaller, easier for her to reach, and although his hands went behind him trying to grab hold of her, she had him exactly where she wanted him.

Part of her wanted to turn him round, pummel him, punch after punch. As she looked over his shoulder, she saw her colleague, down to her underwear but clearly looking relieved. The man eventually succumbed, falling to the ground and Kirsten made her way over to untie the bonds that held Carrie-Anne. She stripped the gag off last, a precaution to make sure she didn't scream if Kirsten untied something the wrong way.

The Welsh woman stood up, shook out her arms and her legs.

'He tore my clothing. Do you think he looks my size?'

Kirsten nodded and the pair quickly bent over the man, untying his shoes, taking his trousers down, and pulling his top off. Carrie-Anne quickly dressed and as Kirsten signalled to her that they needed to leave the room, she grabbed Kirsten, shook her head, and stepped over the man in front of her. Without warning, she kicked him several times, right in the crotch. Kirsten nearly panicked when she saw the man begin to stir, but Carrie-Anne dropped down, driving one knee into his crotch first of all, and then pummelling him with several punches to the face. The man's face turned to one side, clearly unconscious, but still, Carrie-Anne bent to his ear. 'If I had time,' she said, 'I'd rip it off.' And with that, she stood, nodded to Kirsten, and started to make her way out of the room.

Kirsten put her hand up and signalled down the stairs. Slowly, she stepped along, but as she made her way down, she could hear the front door opening. Kirsten's hand went inside her jacket, taking out her weapon and training it towards the front door. She leant in on the stairs, but the man who came in didn't even look up, simply shut the door behind him and walked on through the corridor to make his way to the kitchen.

Kirsten held her ground on the stairs, listening as she heard a kettle boil. Carefully, she made her way down the stairs, Carrie-Anne following, both keeping to the edges so as the stairs would not creak. She wondered if the man would notice her muddy footprints at the back door, or would he think they were from his colleague? If he was clever enough, he'd realise that Kirsten's shoe size was much smaller than the average man. After all, she wasn't much over five feet in height.

Entering the corridor at the bottom of the stairs, Kirsten made her way along to the kitchen door and held her gun at it, while nodding Carrie-Anne to pass behind her. The two women carefully made their way out into the rain. Kirsten signalled towards the hedge at the rear as she closed the door behind her, only just in time before she heard the kitchen door open. Kirsten swung round and put herself up against the wall of the house, indicating Carrie-Anne to do the same. The rear door opened. Behind it, Kirsten had her gun in her hand. She watched the man walk out, yawn, look this way and that out towards the hedge before making his way back in. When the door closed, Kirsten sprinted for the hedge. In contrast to how she arrived, Kirsten with Carrie-Anne in tow did not stop running until they were well clear. Kirsten continued across fields until she got to a point beside the main road and sat down. Carrie-Anne collapsed beside her. Kirsten sucked in the night air, relieved at what she had done. Then she heard the woman beside her begin to sniff.

'Are you okay?' asked Kirsten. 'Did they—?'

Carrie-Anne shook her head. 'He was going to. His boss beat me up. Asked questions, questions about the diamond. Who had it, where it was going, who else was involved? I got the feeling they were contracted.'

'And then what?' said Kirsten.

'His boss went for a sleep. That's when the guy decided he was going to have fun. You got there just in time. Thank you,' said Carrie-Anne. She leant over, putting her head on Kirsten's shoulder. Kirsten wasn't used to this sort of gratitude or even to this sort of trauma, but she opened up her arms and took Carrie-Anne's head into her bosom, holding her close. She'd always thought of Carrie-Anne as the more experienced of the pair of them, but then a situation like this, well, it could be enough to break any woman, or man for that matter. She pulled her phone from her cargo trousers and as she continued to hold Carrie-Anne, she placed a call to Dom.

'This is Dom. What's your status?'

'Got her, Dom. I got her. Down the road from where I left, half a mile. Send somebody to pick us up.'

'Is she okay?'

'Bit battered, bit bruised, but she's okay.'

Kirsten put the phone down and then looked at the woman she was holding in her arms. She wasn't okay. It had clearly terrified her, the thought of what the man was going to do. Kirsten thought that Anna would probably chastise her for going after Carrie-Anne, since she had told her that London wanted them after the diamond, but sitting there in the rain, holding her colleague close, she knew she'd made the right call.

Carrie-Anne suddenly sat up.

'Dom's on his way, is he?' she asked. Kirsten nodded. 'Well, guess we better get back to looking the part. Can't let the boys see us like this. Thank you,' she said. Kirsten nodded. It was time to get back to work.

Chapter 11

irsten sat at the far end of the large table in the back room of the Inverness office. Her team of three sat before her, looking at their boss' expression, wondering where she was about to go with the information she'd received.

'What does this mean then?' asked Kirsten. 'Where are we at?'

'Well,' said Carrie-Anne, 'those who kidnapped me were quite clearly professional, sent over we believe by Kian Furrer, the Swiss collector. They didn't talk when the police pulled them in. As I said, professionals. Most of them escaped as well, but one man was left unconscious in the house. The police said he had severe bruising around the groin area.' Carrie said this with a smile, but Dominic seemed to be a little bit more squeamish about the subject.

'But where does this get us?' repeated Kirsten. 'I've had Anna on the phone asking for an update. What do I tell her after a shootout in Strathpeffer? We have nothing. She's not going to be happy with that.'

'But we've not got nothing,' said Dominic. 'If you look at it, we had this Arab man who's disappeared off. We need to be able to track him. We had the vehicle number, it's been traced further north, but we've also got the diamond on the move chased by James Hutchinson. He's clearly after it as well. He may know a lot more than we do.'

'We may have been playing this wrong,' said Carrie-Anne and the blonde woman stood up, put both hands on the table, and looked down along it towards Kirsten. 'We're the Secret Services, maybe we should keep this secret. Act less like the police.'

'How do you mean?' said Kirsten.

'Well, we got a tip-off, we came in, we surrounded it like we're going to take everyone in, book them, go through proper procedure, but what's our goal here? Our goal here is to get that diamond, whatever it looks like, back to its original owner. Everything else is pretty irrelevant, isn't it? All the other diamonds, whether or not we lift anyone, it all doesn't matter.'

'Point being?' asked Kirsten.

'The point being,' said Carrie-Anne, 'that we should become like one of them.'

'I'm sorry?'

'Look, boss, we need to become like one of these people chasing the diamond. We don't hang about. Let's get in, rough up the others who are after it. We take no prisoners. We just go for what we want. Part of you is almost acting as if we can pick other people up on the fly. Our task was to get that diamond back into the hands of the original owners. Nothing more, nothing less. To be quite frank, I'm not sure London cares who gets left in the wake of this. Their bigger issue is that some foreign power is likely to start taking matters into their own hands on our soil. If we fail, and that actually happens, the four of us can meet down the road at the job centre.'

Dominic sat back in his chair, his hands in front of him, thumbs twiddling. 'Why don't we go after Hutchinson?'

'Why?' asked Kirsten.

'He's clearly got eyes on the prize. He is after it. He's got as many contacts as we have, if not more. He's in the criminal underworld, and more than that, we know him. These other parties, professionals coming in from our Swiss player, Arab gentlemen, sending their own parties in to look at things, we don't know who they are. We know Hutchinson. We have intel on Hutchinson. We can work Hutchinson over.'

'Have you got a plan how to do that?'

'Give me half an hour with Justin. I'll get one sorted for you.'

'Okay. Okay. Bring it to me. I'll decide if it's a goer.'

Dominic stood up, gave a nod to Justin to leave the room with him. The two made their way out.

Kirsten went to get out of her own chair to make her way back to her office, but Carrie-Anne was still standing with her arms on the desk.

'Do you mind if I speak freely, girl to girl?' said Carrie-Anne.

'Always,' said Kirsten, 'you're my team, you have my ear.'

'The thing is, boss, you arrive, and I say to people, "Where do you think she's from?" The majority of this service, do you know what they'd say?'

'What?'

'Police. You act like you're still part of the police. You looked shocked when I kicked that guy in the groin in the farmhouse. We're working with bad people here, properly bad at times, and it's dangerous, and sometimes we've got to get a bit more streetwise. We can't come in like the police. Sometimes you've got to be more ruthless.'

Kirsten sat back in the chair, her mind winding back to the first time she had had to kill someone. She had always said to herself she wouldn't do something unless she had to, and she'd never terminate a life lightly.

'You look conflicted,' said Carrie-Anne, 'and I get it. I know. I had a daughter once. I had a life back in the valleys that was taken away from me by someone, someone I didn't even know. That's just me.'

'I know, I read your file,' said Kirsten.

'No, you don't know. You don't know at all,' said Carrie-Anne, suddenly standing up, 'I suffered, suffered badly at the hands of people that didn't care. They made me suffer. Do you understand that? They actually made me suffer. Last night, I went back into the same scenario. I was measured in there. I could have killed that guy, but I certainly wasn't going to act like a policeman and simply arrest him and haul him in for what he'd done.'

'So, where's your line? asked Kirsten. 'Where do you draw the line?'

'Getting the job done,' said Carrie-Anne. 'That's the line. That's what we're here for, just getting the job done, but for what it's worth, Dominic agrees with me. Dominic says very little, but he knows how to work. He knows when you have to be on the other side, dancing across that line. Sometimes you have to fight fire with fire, Kirsten.'

Kirsten stood almost primly, pulled down her fleece top, and made her way back to her office. She was going to call Anna but what Carrie said was running through her head. She knew she could fight, knew she could handle herself, but this was something else. This was where you blurred the lines to get it done. Macleod never would have had that. The man was by the book. He was solid. Her former boss wouldn't have tolerated something like this. Maybe that's why he didn't work in the intelligence community. Maybe that's why he wasn't here.

Twenty minutes later, Kirsten found herself still pondering these thoughts when there was a rap at the door. It opened, and Dominic marched in with Justin Chivers.

'I think we know how to do it. I need your authorisation though. We need to acquire a boat for tonight and arrange a little meeting with Mr. Hutchinson.'

'How are you going to do that?' asked Kirsten.

'Well,' said Dominic, 'I'll take a seat and run you through it, shall I?'

* * *

Dominic looked up at the rather palatial house in front of him. There were at least six or seven rooms inside. Through one of the windows, he could see a large snooker table and a mammoth TV on the far wall. It might have been one of those romper rooms. Who knew? What Dominic did know was that James Hutchinson was not at home, but his wife most certainly was. Dominic was dressed in shorts and a red top. He had a red jacket over it as well with postal service markings. He'd identified who the postman was for the area, realised there would be at least another thirty minutes to an hour before they would arrive at the house, thereby allowing Dominic to pay a call.

He marched up to the front door, pressed the doorbell, and then found it being opened by a woman in her late forties. She was tall with a narrow nose and looked like she would take no nonsense off anyone. Then again, she was married to James Hutchinson and she'd need to have been made of tough stuff to have been with him this long. He apparently had five kids but who knew what the arrangement was with his wife. Maybe she just turned a blind eye to who he was, accepted the money. Maybe she was in partnership with him but hopefully, she would certainly have his ear.

'Hello, love,' said Dominic as she opened the door, handing over a package, 'I'm sorry but I'm going to need you to sign for this if that's all right?' He took one of the little pads carried by the Post Office and turned it towards the woman. She reached down taking the plastic pencil that wrote on the screen and signed her name.

'What is it?' she asked.

'A special package. It's for Mr. Hutchinson but you could probably have a look inside yourself.'

The woman's face darkened. 'What do you mean?'

'Let's say it's from an interested party, an interested party that wants to meet him.'

'Why should my husband respond to something like this? Do you know who he is?'

Dominic nodded his head. 'Oh, yes, I know who he is,' he said, 'but he doesn't know who we are, but we know what he's after. You can tell him that the photographs of that young girl and him will be displayed in the paper tomorrow if he doesn't come tonight.'

'You're picking on the wrong man with this,' she said.

'Oh no, I think I'm picking on the right one. Just make sure he gets it,' said Dominic. He turned and walked away from the front door. Justin had made a brilliant job of the faked photographs. The only fear on Dominic's mind was she would summon someone from inside. There was bound to be someone around the house, someone who would take care of the family during the day. James Hutchinson was too well despised by certain people not to have protection for his family. If that person walked out with a gun and simply shot him there and then, well, that would be that. Not that Dominic was overly worried. There was a van across the street. It didn't have the Post Office markings on it, instead, it was simple and grey with a window in the back that was darkened. On the other side of that window was Carrie-Anne with a rifle and silencer, ready to take out anyone who threatened Dominic. She stayed there until he had left the street with the message delivered.

* * *

Kirsten had always liked the Caledonian Canal and had been on it several times, cruising along, but never did she think she would steal one of the boats used by one of the companies to hire out to tourists. They were sitting at the jetty at the bottom of the castle at Drumnadrochit, awaiting the arrival of James Hutchinson. On board the boat was Kirsten and Dominic, with Justin Chivers in contact from a van on the far side of the loch, Carrie-Anne was positioned a little distance further down the loch in a black RIB.

A small cavalcade of cars turned up and parked at the top of the castle, five cars in total. Eight men including Hutchinson made their way down past the side of the castle to the small jetty that was often used by the canal boats when the tourists wanted to visit the castle. As they got closer, Dominic, masked by a balaclava, stepped out from the boat on the jetty, produced a torch and shone it in the face of James Hutchinson.

'You can put that bloody thing down. Look, son, give me the photos and we're done.'

'No, we're not,' Dom said. Hutchison nodded to his men and several of them pulled out guns pointing them at Dominic. Dominic turned around and shone a light at the boat where Kirsten was sitting with a large machine gun on her lap pointed directly at Hutchison's party.

'If you'd accompany us, Mr. Hutchinson. There's no need to worry your people; you'll be safely back in no time.'

'What do you mean?' Then Kirsten heard one of Hutchison's men saying, 'Boss, you can't go.'

'Mr. Hutchinson, I'm waiting. In thirty seconds' time, my colleague will open fire. Anybody moves before that, and she'll do it right away. You have things we need to know but to be honest, we can probably find them out from someone else. It'll be a little bit more difficult but if we're finding it out from someone else, you won't know we're finding it out, as you won't be around.'

Hutchinson walked forward. Slowly, he stepped on board the boat with Dominic close behind him. Dominic frisked him, took a gun out from his jacket, and threw it onto the jetty before patting him down and taking a knife out from his ankle. Once he'd done that, Dominic started the boat. He piloted it away from the castle with Kirsten keeping her machine gun the whole time aimed at Hutchinson's men on the jetty.

Dominic piloted the boat into the middle of the loch, at which point, he switched off the engine, and turned off all the lights. He then made Hutchison stand at the rear of the boat which was open to the air but both Kirsten and he stayed inside the cabin with the door open and a gun pointing at

Hutchinson.

'You don't think this is going to work, do you? I'll find you. I'll cut you down,' said Hutchinson.

'Just shut up,' said Dominic, 'until you're asked a question. Diamonds? Where are the diamonds?'

'What diamonds?' said Hutchinson.

'We were there,' said Dominic. 'We were there in Strathpeffer. Your men were going for the diamonds. Your money, your men disappeared with diamonds. Diamonds went everywhere, but we want them, we want them bad.'

'Are you working for the Arabs?' asked Hutchinson. 'I could pay you more.'

'You don't have it then, do you?' said Dominic.

Hutchinson turned away. Kirsten made her way forward and put a gun under Hutchinson's chin. 'They don't do it like we do it here,' said Kirsten. 'I don't particularly think they're gentlemen. I have my orders, I get nothing from you, you end up in the bottom of Loch Ness. It's not what I want, too messy by half. We'll have to scupper this boat as well, so make it easy on you and me; where are your diamonds?'

Hutchinson was starting to quiver now, but he was putting up a front.

'My men will be on that side, they can use a rifle as well. They'll soon take you out from over there.'

'No, they won't,' said Dominic. 'I have people on this side, plenty, watching them. Anybody puts a rifle near here will get a bullet in the brain before they can even fire. We're not some poxy outfit, a couple of clowns running around with a stolen boat.'

Kirsten tried her best not to laugh because it felt like this was exactly what they were.

'Okay, there's not much to tell you, anyway. Yes, I'm after the diamonds, especially the one with the green tinge. It has a name though, but I can't pronounce it. We don't know who has it either, but the Swiss collector Furrer is after it, so it must be good. My man made off with a couple of the diamonds once everything got spilled, but somebody else took the big one. Last I heard they were heading north. My man's on them, that's all I know. Now, if you don't mind, I'll have my pictures.'

Kirsten kept the gun underneath his chin. 'You expect me to go back with that?'

'It's all I've got,' said Hutchinson.

Kirsten put her gun down and took out her knife placing it underneath the man's neck. 'I might have to show them some evidence that I tried.' With that, she let the knife slide down his front, descending towards his waist. 'Over there they cut things off sometimes; did you know that? If you're a thief, you can lose your hands in some of these places. They see it as fair. Maybe your wife would see it as fair if I did a similar sort of thing?'

'You overstepped the mark when you brought my wife into it,' said Hutchinson. 'She knows who I am, but she's good and loyal. She won't care if it goes in the papers.'

'No, but you will,' said Dominic. 'You will because every hope of actually climbing out of the mire you're in and pretending you are something will have gone. What else do you know?' Kirsten moved the knife lower.

'Nothing,' said Hutchinson, 'nothing.' Kirsten could detect the first squeak of fear in his voice, she pressed the knife in close. 'Look, I know nothing,' he said out loud. Kirsten never thought she would see a grown man cry, but Hutchinson had started. 'Just don't. Just don't,' he shrieked.

Kirsten looked over at Dominic, who nodded indicating he felt they'd had everything from the man they were going to get. It appeared he was as much in the dark about who had the large diamond, as anyone else, but his man was on the trail of it, so maybe they should let him go but keep a close eye.

Kirsten tapped her microphone twice and there was the sound of a small engine coming up close to the side of the boat, on the dark side away from the castle. Kirsten grabbed Hutchinson by the hair and kneed him in his groin. He collapsed onto the deck of the boat.

'That's for whatever girl you were doing it with, and for your wife as well.' With that she jumped off into the RIB, followed by Dominic, and Carrie-Anne took them over to the far side. Within five minutes they had deflated the RIB, thrown it in the back of the van, and were disappearing out of the area. In the morning, the police would be told about a missing boat taken from the yards at the start of the Caledonian Canal. It would be found adrift in Loch Ness and Hutchinson would be found nowhere near it.

Chapter 12

Once again, the team were gathered around the conference room in the Inverness office, summoned by Justin Chivers. Kirsten was late into the meeting because she'd just taken a phone call from Anna Hunt. The woman wasn't livid, but there was a distinct cold tone to the happenings at Strathpeffer and Kirsten was quite clear the pressure was now on to recover this diamond.

London, according to Anna, was now worried that the threat was distinctly imminent from one of the Middle Eastern countries, which indicated that Anna thought the wrong people had got hold of the diamond. Where they were taking it was up for grabs but needed to be found out straightaway. Kirsten relayed this message to the team before looking at Justin, wondering why he had pulled them in.

'I've been on the wires checking through contacts. Specifically, we've been looking at Hutchinson's men, through phone taps and a few of the other guys I have out and about. They keep their noses to the grindstone, they don't ruffle any feathers, and it's just words and contacts. But there's a move up north, I believe there may be something going down in Tain.'

'Tain?' queried Kirsten. 'Why on earth would you go up to Tain?'

'I think it's where Hutchinson's man went. He definitely had word from Hutchinson, although we didn't know what it was that was said, and he's ended up in Tain. So, either he's gone up there because that's where he believes the bigger diamond is or he's been instructed to do that by Hutchinson.'

'But we don't know the reason,' said Dominic. 'This could be a wild goose chase.'

'It could be a wild goose chase,' said Justin, 'but at the moment we don't have a lot of geese to chase. And from what the boss has just said, London's going to get pretty rough with us if we don't follow everything up.'

'I didn't say we shouldn't follow it,' said Dominic, 'but I wouldn't send all our assets.' He flashed a glance at Kirsten, who nodded.

'Agreed,' she said, 'but if it's going to be something important, it needs to be more than one of us. Dominic, you and Carrie-Anne head up to investigate. I'll stay here in case something bigger breaks. Justin, get your ears back on the jungle drums and find out what's going on. And have we got a tail on Hutchinson?'

'I've got three different people watching Hutchinson,' said Justin Chivers.

'How are you doing that?' asked Dominic. 'He's not the easiest person to keep a tail on, especially now he knows he's probably being watched.'

'For this room only,' said Justin, 'I have three people within his organisation. They're on the edge, they're low level, and they don't get fed a lot, but that which they do, they send to me.'

'When did we get them in there?'

'Long term sleeping assets,' said Justin. 'Anna had them installed a long time ago. They don't raise their head and they're in parts of the business that mean Hutchinson wouldn't even know who they are, but it's amazing what gets said and what gets overheard. Especially if you can give people a few odd devices to help them along.'

Kirsten almost laughed. When she'd first met Justin Chivers, she'd thought he was a bit of a clown. Quite a pervy man, there just to see what skirt he could pick, but he was turning into something rather different and there was something else about him, something she couldn't put a finger on.

'Head up to Tain, find out what's going on. You're authorised to act and act fast if needs be. But we keep our persona as the other side, the people searching, not as law enforcement. I think that's the best way to run.'

'I think that's for the best too,' said Carrie-Anne, 'I'll just go and get changed.' She stood up once again in an immaculate skirt, blouse, and jacket and strode out of the room in high heels. Justin glanced over at her, and Kirsten watched him closely. There was something just not right about the way he looked at her. It was almost as if he was obliged. Men didn't look at women like it was an obligation. They did enjoy it, the same way she enjoyed a good-looking man, but she was struggling to see that from Justin. It had taken her a while to pick up on it, and only now she watched him closely.

'Let's see what we can get you, boss,' said Dominic, rising from his chair. 'We'll not be long.'

* * *

Dominic stood in a large coat in front of the counter, taking in the smell that was assaulting his nose. Chips were always delightful, cooked in the hot fat from the deep fryers in front of him, but unfortunately someone had gone and put vinegar on them, and it had passed across the front of him on the way to another customer.

Carrie-Anne was waiting at the back of the shop. Her hair was tied up in a bandana and she was wearing a t-shirt with the name of a band she didn't even recognise. Her torn jeans and Doc Martin boots finished the look, along with the chain that was hanging around her waist. She wore no makeup and chewed some gum. Deep inside she knew her mother would be disgusted.

Dominic watched the person with the vinegar chips leave the building and turned round to look at Carrie-Anne. He gave a nod and she stood up, coming over towards him. She snaked a leg around his and put her arm around his shoulder.

'You want to buy me a supper?'

'What the hell!' said Dominic. 'What you playing at?'

Earlier that day, Dominic had found a source of Justin Chivers who had relayed that there was a meeting that night in the fish and chip shop on a street in the middle of Tain. It would take place at approximately eight o'clock upstairs. Having recced the building, Dominic had observed the front door, which they used to enter the fish and chip shop, and one rear door, which for some reason, somebody had stuck a large bin in front of at this time, rendering it useless for escape. The fish and chip shop was not the most salubrious, and certainly wasn't doing a roaring trade. Now that the man who liked vinegar on his chips had left, there was only Dominic and Carrie-Anne inside.

'Would you get off me, woman?' said Dominic as Carrie-Anne ran a hand across his face.

'I think someone needs a little bit of loving, what'd you think?' said Carrie-Anne, leaning back, shaking her chest in front of Dominic.

Dominic turned to the man behind the counter. 'What the hell does this mean? Is she in here often?'

The man shook his head. 'Hey love, leave him alone.'

'Piss off. I can tell when a man wants it. Probably pay for it too. That's these upper-class types, always like this.' And with that Carrie-Anne ran her hand down Dominic's front. Dom grabbed her wrist, stopping it short of his crotch. 'Mate, would you come around and do something about her? Otherwise, I'm going to have to. I don't like to hit a woman.'

'I don't hit women either,' said the man. 'Look, love, have some chips and clear off.'

'I don't want chips. I want this man, and he wants me. Can't you tell?'

'I'm going to phone the police in a minute,' said Dominic. 'I'm going to bring the police in here. Look, would you just get her off me?'

The man behind the counter shook his head, exited from behind the counter into another room before coming round and opening a door behind Dominic and Carrie-Anne. Like a whippet, Carrie-Anne went for the man and grabbed him in a choke with one hand. Dominic looked around the chippy and found a small unit, which he placed beside the door. There was no way anyone was getting out of this building. Carrie-Anne continued to hold the man by the neck, her height allowing her to drive him through the access door he had come through. Once there she saw the stairs and marched the man up them and around several corners, until she pulled him close.

'Where are they?' she said in a whisper. The man shook his head.

'I said, where are they?' Again, the man shook his head. They'd gone up two flights of stairs now, and Carrie-Anne took the man, pushed him over the edge of the balustrade, holding him by his neck, his waist on the balustrade so that he was at balance but precarious, ready to tumble down the gap in the middle of the stairs.

'I really don't give a damn about you, sunshine. All I want is my diamond. Where is it?'

The man looked out of the corner of his eye at a door further up the stairs. 'Thank you,' said Carrie-Anne, and still holding him by the throat, pulled him back off the banister and threw him into the wall, his head contacting with it, causing the man to fall down. Dominic checked to see if the man was out cold, and once happy that he was, he nodded at Carrie-Anne to continue up the stairs.

The noise of bouncing the proprietor off the wall had caused the door at the top to be opened, and Carrie-Anne heard an expletive before it was shut firmly. Dominic could hear a lock being turned and pulled out his silenced weapon from inside his jacket. He fired several shots into the lock, hearing screams from inside, carried on, and kicked the door, which rebounded and opened, providing a view of the scene inside.

There was a table with three men around it. One looked large, as if he could handle himself, one looked extremely scared, and the other they recognised from that night at Strathpeffer.

'Where are our diamonds?' said Carrie-Anne. 'Give them now, and we might let you live.'

'Like hell,' said the large man. 'These belong to Mr. Hutchinson. Until he gets money for them, they're going nowhere.' The man stepped forward, raised his fist, but Dominic held up his gun. 'And you're going to do what with that? Sit down, tiny.'

Carrie-Anne walked over to the man who was looking at the diamonds intently and then pointed her finger at the man from Strathpeffer. 'You, sit your ass down. And you, how good are these diamonds?'

The man looked at her. 'Don't you know? I mean, these are top quality.'

Top quality, thought Carrie-Anne, *and yet they left them to go after that one single diamond.* 'Put them in the bag,' said Carrie-Anne.

'I can't do that. They don't belong to me,' said the man. Carrie-Anne took the butt of her gun and smacked the man across the face, causing him to fall off the chair.

'That's fine,' she said, and then turned the gun and pointed at the man from Strathpeffer. 'You put them in it.' The man nodded eagerly, reached forward, and swept them all into a small bag on the table.

Dominic stepped forward to the large man, who was now sitting down. 'You look like you can handle yourself, but you've been good, in fairness, so I won't hit you too hard, just enough so you won't follow me. Then, after that, I'd suggest you run, because Mr. Hutchinson will be wanting a word with you.' Dominic could see the man's shocked face but hit him across the head with a gun butt, causing him to slump over the chair. He was clearly still conscious though, so Dominic hit him again.

'I'm doing nothing,' said the man from Strathpeffer. 'I got

them here, that was my responsibility. All this, not my fault. You won't get any hassle from me.'

Carrie-Anne put her gun in the man's face. 'You're right we won't. There's somebody watching this place. You'll be followed when you come out. If anybody else gets wind of who we are within the next two hours, you won't see the night. Do you understand me? You're in the big boys' leagues now.'

The man nodded, and Carrie-Anne almost let out a laugh. Dominic took the diamonds and made his way out of the door down into the ground floor of the chippy. He could feel his stomach rumbling. 'Have we got time for a—?'

Carrie-Anne looked across at him. 'No, we don't!'

They walked out of the front door, but Dominic looked before his departure, sighing at the small array of battered sausages, fish, and steakettes that lay inside the fryer. He glanced back to the door, but Carrie-Anne had already gone through. Quickly, he jumped across the counter. Leaning around, he slid back the door of the heated area on top of the fryer. He picked up a battered sausage and slid the cover back again. Quickly, he made his way out onto the street, where he saw a look from Carrie-Anne. 'Sorry,' he said. 'I didn't think you wanted any.'

'I cannot believe that you stopped for a sausage.'

'Well, we're still going to drive back, then we'll get these looked at. It could be a reasonably long evening, but I'll tell you what, while I'm enjoying it, I'll let you call the boss with the good news.'

Carrie-Anne looked behind her. No one was coming out of the door of the fish and chips shop. 'Come on, let's get in the car,' she said. 'I don't feel right without a bit of mascara.'

Chapter 13

On their return from Tain, Dominic had gone straight to bed, crashing out in the back room of the team's offices in Inverness. Carrie-Anne, on the other hand, had waited up for the diamond expert to arrive. The man hadn't been advised of where the diamonds came from, or any of the backstory around them, but he was a trusted colleague of the service. He would come in, do his job by giving his thoughts on the items laid before him and then promptly leave, forgetting he was ever there.

Kirsten walked into the conference room at the rear of the offices and saw Carrie-Anne, dressed as ever in a neat skirt with heels and jacket. Beside her was a small man with round glasses, who brought his own light to the table. Underneath that light was held one of the diamonds and he was examining it closely with an eyeglass.

'Any luck with it?' asked Kirsten when she came in.

She saw the little man turn around and take a look up and down at her. He seemed to almost dismiss her and went back to looking at the diamonds. Maybe it was the black cargo trousers she was wearing or the simple T-shirt over the top. Carrie-Anne certainly cut more of the office boss figure and with Kirsten being younger as well, the man could be forgiven for not recognising she was the one who had called him in.

'I said, do we have any luck?'

'Mr. Adams here is still looking, boss,' said Carrie-Anne at which point the man almost choked, before putting his eyepiece down, turning around, and walking serenely over to Kirsten extending a hand.

'They're fine diamonds,' said Mr. Adams. 'The majority of them would be worth a reasonable amount of money but they're nothing special. They're not unique like the one you were asking me to look for.'

Kirsten could see the man staring up and down at her attire and then up to her hair, which currently she had tied back. 'Dom's down below sleeping,' said Carrie-Anne. 'Thought he could grab a nap while we got this checked through.'

'You could have as well. You should've called me,' said Kirsten. 'I'd have looked after Mr. Adams. Please, sir, don't let me stop you getting back to your task.'

Carrie-Anne stepped to one side with Kirsten, allowing the little man to take to the table again and muse over the stones that were there.

'Where else are we?' asked Kirsten in a whisper.

'Not far at all to be honest, boss. If the stone isn't here, we're not sure where the rest have gone. We've tailed Hutchinson and his men. So far, all we've come up with is finding some more of the diamonds. As for the one that was taken by the foreign gentleman, we're not sure where it is. Unless Justin has got some feelers out.'

'I think Hutchinson is still the one to watch. It may be up to Justin to get our next deal.'

'What do we do, boss, if that doesn't come through?'

'Well, you can get down to the Job Centre first,' said Kirsten. 'They're always looking for a smart-dressed woman.'

Carrie-Anne laughed. Then her face became serious again.

'I don't know what we're going to do,' said Kirsten. 'Anna Hunt was on again. London this, London that. Maybe London should get their arses up here.'

'London's tone,' asked Carrie-Anne, 'has it become more worried?'

'How do you mean?' asked Kirsten.

'Is it becoming more paranoid, panicky? The thing is these diamonds have been picked up by some Arab men. If it's the wrong one, the likelihood of the other Arab country taking action, that's going to increase. That will get London very nervous.'

'I can see why you're an analyst,' said Kirsten. 'For the record, they do sound like they're getting more worried. Although it's been distilled through the even tones of Anna. She never shows much.'

'True,' said Carrie-Anne, 'but even Anna will start to shiver and shake, so to speak.'

The little man at the desk continued for another ten minutes before waving the women over. He pulled out a seat for Kirsten, which she felt was a nice touch. As she sat down, he drew one of the diamonds over towards her.

'Look at it, absolutely stunning,' he said. 'Absolutely stunning, but not unique. Every single one of these diamonds is worth a small fortune, but you could replace them with another one. You asked me to look for something of uniqueness. It's not here.'

'Thank you, Mr. Adams,' said Kirsten. 'Carrie-Anne, would you escort Mr. Adams back outside?'

'Anytime,' he said. Once again, Kirsten got the feeling he was giving her a strange look. As he made it to the door, he tilted his head back. 'The last person who was in here,' he said, 'he was much more well-attired.'

'Would have been a while back then,' said Kirsten. 'New rules new ways. You know how it goes.'

The little man clearly didn't, but he nodded anyway and shuffled his way out of the room. Carrie-Anne took a look at Kirsten, giving a face that said, 'Well, I never' before following the man and taking him to the front door of the office. Kirsten continued to sit on her seat, threw her feet up onto the table in front of her, and began to ponder. As much as she hated it, they were now in the arms of Justin Chivers. Could he find a contact? Was he able to work out where the diamonds were going? Kirsten hated that it was like this.

Back in the day, she'd have been on the computer, sitting there with Ross, chugging away through the minutiae. Now, she had to take a more hands-off role. She had her communications man, a computer expert who would delve into things. While she could easily cover off what he was doing, he did have a level that was beyond her. Besides, there were too many other things to look at, now she was the boss. That word, it still didn't sit with her. Kirsten looked around for coffee and found that the cafetière was empty.

She made her way over to the little table at the side of the conference room, switched the kettle on, and tipped out some coffee into the cafetière. As she waited for the kettle to boil, she found herself staring at the wall. Though her eyes were looking there, her mind was wandering elsewhere. The driver down in London. She couldn't get him out of her head, but she wondered, *Was it him? Or was it just the time to sit and talk with someone?* She couldn't do that anymore. She had met Macleod, her old boss, but all she'd been able to say was, 'Thank you,' but she couldn't tell him for what. Even meeting Hope in this case, it wasn't the same. She didn't have the team feel. She wasn't one of them anymore.

There came a knock at the door and Kirsten jerked out of her daydream, spun around, and saw Justin Chivers staring at her.

'You look trim in those cargo pants.'

Kirsten simply shook her head. Something was not right about the man. For all his quips, she was getting the feeling that too many of them were becoming forced.

'What is it, Justin?'

'I've had word. One of the tails on Hutchinson has him headed for a cruise ship up in Aberdeen.'

'Cruise ship in Aberdeen, which cruise ship?'

'*Her Majesty's Pride,*' said Justin. 'It's the biggest cruise ship in the world. They're up there doing their try-out runs. Usually works out of Southampton, but they're doing a run up to Aberdeen, Shetland, round to the Western Isles. Got some passengers on board, but it's not fully loaded.'

'Hutchinson is going on board since when?'

'Well, he's headed up that way, should be there by this afternoon. I checked through the records of the company. They've got a Mr. and Mrs. Hutchinson, all above board. It appears he paid for it as well with his own money.'

'So, what's he doing? Is he chasing the diamonds? Do you think they're going on the cruise ship or is he just taking the Mrs. for a bit of TLC to make up for us storming in at the door?'

'I don't think his wife gets too much TLC and besides he

probably wouldn't be taking her. I doubt this is anything of kindness from him. I think he's after the diamond; he must know something.'

'Have you had any other leads? Any other chatter?'

'Nothing,' said Justin, 'but he was keen on it. Wasn't he?'

The door of the room opened, and Carrie-Anne strode in. Looking over his shoulder, Justin gave a long stare at Carrie-Anne's legs, his lips blowing out to the point where Kirsten thought a wolf whistle would follow. Again, it was totally out of context in the middle of the conversation they were having, Kirsten was feeling a little off-balance with his act now.

'What's up?' asked Carrie-Anne

'Justin reckons that Hutchinson's going to get on a cruise ship up in Aberdeen. *Her Majesty's Pride.*'

'The new one,' said Carrie-Anne. 'That's like the biggest cruise ship in the world. Isn't it? It's not ready yet though.'

'No, but it's running its sea and passenger trials at the moment. What do you reckon?' Kirsten asked Carrie-Anne.

'It does seem a bit strange, doesn't it? Going off on a cruise when you're in middle of chasing a diamond like this. It might be a way to get it out of the country though as well.'

'I think we need to be on board. Justin, sort it out, but we'll need to go in disguise. See if you can get Dom and Carrie-Anne in as a couple and then you'll need to get me in as well, but make sure I'm in the lower down accommodation. I want Carrie-Anne and Dom up top, somewhere close to Hutchinson.'

'If you want, I can come as well. We could pose as a couple.'

Kirsten shook her head. 'No, I need to be on my own and I need somebody out here to pull the strings. You can't do that from on board. Go and get it sorted for me.'

'Are you sure you don't want to?'

'Justin, go.'

Kirsten watched him shut the door and then Carrie-Anne made way over to her. 'He's a bit of a creep really, isn't he?'

'No, he's not,' said Kirsten. 'I'm not buying it.'

'Why? Because a man's looking at you. Why wouldn't they?'

Kirsten looked at the woman talking to her dressed as neatly as she was. Carrie-Anne carried the look. Then Kirsten looked at herself, the cargo trousers, the t-shirt. She was more at home in a gym than she'd ever be looking like a power-dressed woman.

'It's not that,' said Kirsten. 'He tries too hard. I've never had somebody speak like that to me all the time, and he did it at first when I was on his level. Now I'm the boss, he's still doing it. I never saw him speak to Anna Hunt like that.'

'Anna Hunt probably would've put him up against a wall, tore his manhood away from him.'

'She could have turned around quite easily and clocked him for it had he said it to any other woman.'

Kirsten poured herself coffee, offered one to Carrie-Anne, and then made her way back to her own desk. Once again, she sat looking out the window. She'd find out from Justin when they were on the move but expected it to be very shortly. The cruise ship sounded nice, but a cruise ship alone—she'd have to stop this. Once again, she was going off-track, thinking about private life and not the work that was in front of her.

There was a knock on the door and Justin came in. 'One solo-cabin secured,' he said, 'and a hot bed for the other two.'

Kirsten raised an eye. 'Take a seat, Justin.'

The man came over and Kirsten got up and shut her office door.

'When are we off?'

'You'll need to get up there in about five hours' time. You need to make a move in a couple of hours. I've got you in though, said I was an industry rep. I managed to squeeze a couple of extra spaces. That's pretty normal, anyway. I mean, they like this. Low key, low-level number of passengers so they can get their service right. Just make sure you act as if this is what you're doing. Going on holiday. Make sure you look excited,' said Justin.

'Don't worry. I will do. What's on board it?'

'It's got everything. You've got cinemas. You've got loads of dining rooms. You've got theatre. You've got swimming pools coming out of your backside. Oh, that's a thought,' he said. 'Which bikini are you taking?'

Kirsten couldn't help but feel that there was no conviction there, and she walked around Justin's side of the desk. His chair was a little way out from it, and he was sitting with both feet on the floor. She walked across, suddenly spun and placed herself right on his lap throwing her arm around his neck. His first reaction was to recoil, not in a way that said his dream had finally arrived and he wasn't ready for it, but as if this was not a natural response for him.

'You ever had a woman in this position before?' asked Kirsten. Justin simply stared at her. 'I would have thought you'd have been quite happy now. You really should be lifting your arm and putting it around my back, then you can settle in more comfortably.'

'Anna said you were good,' said Justin, 'and I didn't believe her. She said there was more to you than someone who simply ran around. She said you had the eye for knowing things, to spot people, see through them. What gave me away?'

'You overplayed it with me. Too much, too often. Somebody

like me and a guy like you're meant to be, you would get a little bit worried every now and again. You would be careful when you said things. When you put the tacky comments in, you were throwing them in too keenly.'

'Anna's the only one that knows,' said Justin.

'Is that because there is someone else?'

'There is. Do I need to . . .'

'You don't need to tell me anything. What you do need to do is to write down where he lives, what his name is, seal it all up in an envelope for me, and then tell me where I can find that envelope.'

'Why?' asked Justin.

'Because he's a threat to this department, a liability to us. Also, if you go off the grid or you go missing, I need to know why, and if your partner is being threatened, I need to know where to find him.'

'Okay,' said Justin, 'I will do. Are you going to let the rest of the team know?'

'No,' said Kirsten.

She jumped up off Justin's lap. 'I'm the boss. I have to have my secrets. I expect you to stay in character. Carrie-Anne's an analyst, and she's a darn good one. You break your character and she'll clock it.'

'Yes, boss.'

The man stood up, almost dejected, and started making his way to the door. Kirsten put out a hand and stopped him.

'Justin, it's okay. I know. I'm your new Anna, don't worry about it and good work. We wouldn't be after this diamond, we wouldn't be anywhere near it, without you. You're going nowhere from this team; you're right where you need to be.'

Justin nodded and made his way out of the door.

Part of Kirsten was feeling strange. She suddenly got to look at the life of a spy, a life being undercover, the man who couldn't say what he was, had to pretend to be someone else and had to keep the love of his life tucked away somewhere. She thought about the driver down south. A simple picture when you went out for a coffee and a chat, but if it was to become more, well, did she have to have this type of life too? Keep things covered? Kirsten made her way back to her desk, picked up her car keys, and decided to make her way home. She had clothing to pack; after all, she was a tourist going on a jolly holiday. Time to put the game face on.

Chapter 14

Kirsten arrived at the docks in a ten-year-old green hatchback and pulled a rucksack out from the back, throwing it over her shoulder. At the far side of the check-in area, a taxi pulled up and several cases of luggage were taken out for Dominic and Carrie-Anne. Mr and Mrs. Anderson, as was their cover, had arrived, people with a bit of money and a ton of class, exactly the customers that the top end of the ship needed to satisfy. By contrast, Kirsten was wearing one of her wrestling tops with a massive logo and the picture of some rather dubious figures on the front. She had a leather jacket slung over her shoulder, her hair was loose and a mess, and her hiking boots had a hole developing towards the front.

As she approached the check-in and saw Carrie-Anne, the woman gave her a look of disgust, turning her nose away. Her Welsh colleague was in a pair of long white trousers, heavily flared at the bottom, and wore a set of heels underneath that Kirsten would have fallen over in. Dominic was smartly attired in a neat suit, and a pair of sunglasses that said, 'Don't bother me.'

Kirsten was led via a different gangway to the vessel and she stopped on the quayside, looking at the vast ship. She pulled out a camera and started taking photos. The crewman who was to take her on board tried to usher her along, but he was smiling gracefully the whole time. 'If you'll come this way, ma'am.'

'It's just so big,' said Kirsten. 'I can't believe I'm getting on here. This is fabulous.'

'I see you like the wrestling.'

'Oh,' said Kirsten. 'Yes. So good, isn't it? Do you watch it yourself?'

The man, whose name was Pedro, according to the badge on his chest, nodded enthusiastically. 'I've been to it lots of times,' said Kirsten. 'Every time it's come over here, I've gone. My granny used to go to the old one when they used to have it up and down the country. She'd have hit them with her handbag.'

While her face was giving an excited look, Kirsten's eyes were scanning the boat. The vessel was truly magnificent, and along the side were a myriad of balconies. Kirsten knew that her cabin would be one of the ones towards the bottom. Originally, Justin had arranged for her to have an interior cabin. Kirsten hadn't liked the sound of that, and so she had been granted an upgrade on arrival, just so they could check out how that particular set of cabins was working for people. There was no service, no changing of fruit baskets or any of the other exciting extras Dominic and Carrie-Anne would be enjoying, but with a balcony, Kirsten had access to the outside of the vessel.

As Kirsten made her way up the gangway, she looked across at the rather more salubrious one where Carrie-Anne was followed by Dominic. They were probably arriving to cocktails, maybe even champagne, and part of her felt a little jealous, despite the fact she knew they were still working. Once inside she was greeted and taken to her cabin. Her baggage was brought on board for her, and Kirsten spent the next twenty minutes unpacking.

They were booked onboard for a week. The vessel was to take them all the way down towards Southampton, where Justin had booked a flight back up, just in case things went on that long. Kirsten reckoned she needed to get on top of things quickly. The boat would leave Aberdeen that night and then make a trip towards Orkney before heading north towards Shetland, and although it was traveling slowly, it would still be only two days until it would start letting people go ashore in Shetland. If the diamond was on board now and was being taken north, maybe that would be the place they would drop it off.

You could fly out of Shetland. But then you could fly from Stornoway in the Western Isles and to all the other quick stops it was making on the way down to the Port of Southampton. It was a heck of a task ahead of her, she thought. They didn't even know if the diamond was on board. They didn't know who had it. All they knew was that Hutchinson was making his way on board at a time when he was hunting the diamond furiously.

Kirsten made her way out to the balcony and stood looking at the harbour side. It wasn't very plush and she wondered when they would get underway. Cruise ships were not something that had come across her life previous to this. She wasn't used to how they worked. While she was outside, she tapped her earpiece and called Dominic and Carrie-Anne to check in. Carrie-Anne announced she was loud and clear, but when she spoke to Dom, there were simply two taps, indicating he was currently with someone but couldn't speak.

'I'm going to go up, take a look around the swimming area and the gym,' said Kirsten. 'See who's on board. Take a walk through the large shopping mall and the cafes and the restaurants,' she told Carrie-Anne. 'See who you can see. We'll catch up in about three hours' time.'

Kirsten checked in with Justin who was back at base. Upon finding that the communications were all working well, Kirsten delved into her unpacked clothes, grabbed her training gear and a swimsuit before making her way up to the top levels of the vessel.

Kirsten walked into the gym and was staggered. There was row on row of treadmills, skiing machines, as well as rowing machines with only a couple of people using them. Behind the desk, a woman smiled at her, offering a towel and getting her to sign in before taking her on a small tour. There was a weights area and also a corner with punch bags, everything she had in her gym back home.

Kirsten entered the locker area, was given a key, and quickly changed into her Lycra shorts, a crop top, and her punch gloves. She put a towel around her neck and made her way out to the punch bags, warming up in the corner. She was frustrated. She knew what was coming up, knew it would be difficult, and she felt like they never had a full grasp on what was going on while chasing the diamonds. But now in front of her, a certain bag would suffer for that feeling of despair she had.

The gym also had windows at one side that looked onto a large recreational area where she could see a smoothie shop, other healthy eating options, and a library. From her corner, she was able to look out and see the few people who were milling about. She imagined that in full function, the place would be packed, but Justin said there was less than ten percent of the normal passengers that there would be.

Kirsten put her head down and started to pound the bag in front of her. She went through the routines she had been taught in the gym back home, working the hands and the feet, with half an eye watching the area through the window. It was half an hour in, with sweat dripping off her, that she suddenly realised she recognised someone sitting across in the smoothie bar. She had seen the face briefly back in Strathpeffer when she had popped her head around the corner and a face had looked back at her. That face was now here. It was a white man, brown hair and a moustache, but she'd need to know who he was and what he was doing. She tapped her earpiece.

'Charlie,' she said. There were two taps. 'Charlie, I need you to come up to the smoothie shop, up where the gym is, level below the swimming pools. I think I've clocked someone. I need you to find out who he is, what he's doing. I can't at the moment because I'm stuck in the gym. I want to keep eyes on him in case he moves.'

There were three taps to confirm that the instruction was being actioned. It was five minutes later when Kirsten, still battering away on the bag in front of her, saw Carrie-Anne walking along the small mall outside the gym.

'In front of the smoothie shop. He's got the yellow smoothie in front of him. Moustache, brown hair, white man.'

'Kilo, got it.' And with that, communications were broken off. Kirsten was feeling the effort of having hit this bag for the last forty minutes, and so she stepped away, went back to the locker room, and took a quick shower. She then made her way up one level to the main swimming pool.

There were flumes on one side, several Jacuzzis, a large pool in the middle where you could swim, but which also had rapids in one side. There were also lots of different areas which kids could use. The place was quiet, and when Kirsten went to get changed, she came out to an almost empty pool. She made her way in and swam a couple of lengths before stepping out and making her way over to the sauna.

As she entered, she almost recoiled but kept her composure, holding her towel close to her. In the far corner of the sauna was Hutchinson. Lying in front of him was a woman who wasn't his wife. Kirsten was dressed in a swimsuit because she was practical when she went to the swimming pool. She wasn't on the beach trying to parade her figure; she was there to swim. But this woman lying in front of Hutchinson was clearly there for his enjoyment.

Having stepped into the sauna, Kirsten could hardly step out, so she made her way to the top of it and lay down, putting a towel across her face. It was ten minutes before the man left. Kirsten gave it another two before she stepped out into the cold shower and watched him as he made his way across the pool. The woman who was with him was now lying beside him on a lounger, but Kirsten watched two other men come close to Hutchinson. One, she clocked from Strathpeffer, the other one, she was unsure. She tapped her ear.

'Delta, up in the main swimming pool. Hutchinson's here, he's got two other guys come. I recognise one from Strathpeffer. I think we may have an entire team on board. He certainly must believe that it's here. Do we have any Arab gentlemen on board?'

'We'll need to get the list, find out the crew and also the guests. It could still be six or seven hundred people on board.'

'I was thinking more like fifteen hundred. I'm going to get

on to Juliet, see if he can get true lists sent through to me.'

'Give me two minutes and I'll join you,' said Dominic.

Two minutes later, Kirsten was sitting in a Jacuzzi at the far side of the pool. Dominic arrived, lay down a towel on a lounger and entered the Jacuzzi just across from her. He gave a pleasant smile as if he didn't know her and then laid back, enjoying the bubbles. 'How do we play this?' he said under his breath.

'I get hold of Justin and we find out Arab names and see who they are, who's onboard, anyone of Middle Eastern origin, then we check them out. It was definitely a Middle Eastern man who grabbed the diamond.'

'It could've gone anywhere, though, by now,' said Dominic.

'I doubt it,' said Kirsten. 'If this is the other side and they've grabbed it, they will be trying to get it out of the way. Maybe they sent their own.'

'Okay,' said Dominic. 'What do you want me to do?'

'Keep a tail on Hutchinson. Where he goes, who he speaks to. Get me photographs of everyone he speaks to. Also see if he's hovering close to anyone else we don't know, anyone of foreign descent.'

'Needle in a haystack, really, isn't it?' said Dominic.

'It is indeed,' said Kirsten, and she stepped out of the Jacuzzi, but as she was about to go, she heard a throwaway comment from Dominic. 'Bet you're glad Juliet's not here. Especially going around in a swimsuit like that.'

Kirsten turned around, smiled, and nodded. The man really did have them fooled, didn't he?

Chapter 15

Standing in Dominic and Carrie-Anne's room, Kirsten realised she really had been given the cheap option. The suite was on two floors, bedrooms upstairs, an expansive lounge below which led out onto a balcony. From the living room, Kirsten could see her colleagues. Dominic's arm around Carrie-Anne's waist, watching as they left Aberdeen Harbour. It was a tradition for everyone to be out on their balconies, or up top on deck, as the boat departed a harbour, but Kirsten couldn't be seen out on the balcony for this was not her accommodation. Instead, she was inside gearing up in her black garb awaiting this evening's festivities to start before she would make her move. Carrie-Anne made her way back into the living room and appraised Kirsten.

'Looks good, boss, everything tight, shipshape. Another twenty minutes she should be ready to go.'

Kirsten tapped her ear. 'Comms check.'

'Charlie's on, you're loud and clear.'

'Kilo on, loud and clear as well.'

'Delta loud and clear,' said Dominic entering the room.

'Good,' said Kirsten, looking at Dom in a white tuxedo, a red cummerbund and red bow tie, setting off his look. Carrie-

Anne dazzled in a sparkling dress, her hair looking like she'd been in the hairdresser's all afternoon but in reality, she'd managed to get herself ready within thirty minutes. Kirsten had never had that sort of ability with her hair; it either hung out the back in a ponytail, or it swayed around on its own. That reminded her and she tied up her hair preparing it to be tucked up in the back of the balaclava she had put on.

The plan was to infiltrate Hutchinson's suite while he was out at a gala dinner that night. Dominic and Carrie-Anne would keep their eyes on him making sure that Kirsten didn't get any unwelcome intruders. Outside, darkness had fallen, and Kirsten could see the lights of the harbour disappear slowly and as the ship turned northward, she was gazing out into dark sea. The opposite side of the ship would be looking at the land, the east coast of Scotland, as the vessel made its way up and then over to Orkney where it would perform a short stop without landing anyone ashore. After that, they were off to Shetland where the plan was to take everyone off board on a small tour around the island before returning, getting practice in their offloading and re-boarding techniques.

Kirsten made her way to the balcony, keeping low so none of those on either side could see her, and she felt the wind beginning to whip.

'We're making our way shortly,' said Carrie-Anne and Kirsten turned around holding up her hand in front of her mouth indicating the woman should stay quiet. Kirsten made her way back inside, closed the door behind her before standing up fully. 'Voices carry out there,' said Kirsten, 'too easily, but if you're ready to go, I'll prep myself.

'Are you going in armed?' asked Dominic.

'It's kind of bulky but I will do,' said Kirsten, 'although I've got a few other weapons with me as well. Best if I don't get found out in there.'

'Best indeed,' said Dom and turned around to Carrie-Anne putting out his arm, 'Shall we, my dear?'

Carrie-Anne linked her arm in his and together they made their way out of the suite. The lights were switched off and Kirsten stood in the darkness letting her eyes get accustomed to it. A couple of minutes later she made her way out onto the balcony, keeping down low and seeing if anyone else was out on the balconies on the same level. There was a couple at the far end but after a few moments, they seemed to go inside.

There weren't any balcony lights on, and only one or two of the cabins had their lights shining out from within. Kirsten wasn't worried about that because her plan was to crawl along the ship just above the cabins. There wasn't a lot of room, and she would be high up on the vessel which meant the wind could be a serious factor, but she'd seen a line, a railing of sorts, that she could clip to as she made her way along.

Kirsten remained crouched down until fifteen minutes later when Dom spoke in her ear.

'He's in the room. Kilo is good to go.'

Kirsten climbed up the outside of the door of the cabin until she found the railing high above it. Putting her fingers onto it, she shimmied her way along, counting five cabins, the fifth one of which would be Hutchinson's.

As she made her way along, the door of a cabin beneath opened and Kirsten froze, hanging on to the side. She looked down to see a woman walk out, clearly in some sort of a strop, shortly followed by a man, who the woman didn't look at, continuing to stare off into the sea, something for which Kirsten was thankful. The man put his arms around her, but she shrugged them off and then slowly he started to make more moves of appeasement, rubbing her neck, and stretching round her again.

Kirsten was wary they could turn around, possibly look up and see her, so rather than just remain fixed in her position, she crawled along as quickly as she could until she got to the middle of the balcony beside. Once there, she clung on tight and listened as the couple had a blazing row. They seemed so involved that she continued to crawl along, soon coming to Hutchinson's balcony.

There was no light below so Kirsten let herself down slowly, knowing that the rowing couple had now gone inside. She reached into the lock pick set in her back pocket and examined the door in front of her, and then ever so gingerly she tried the door, realising it was open. Many people would have seen this as a good sign but for Kirsten, she understood her work was really about to begin. An open door probably meant a cabin that wasn't empty, and she'd have to tread carefully.

Delicately, she slid the door back just enough so she could get inside, and then she closed the door again, hoping that any draught that had come in would be unnoticed by the occupant. The layout of the cabin was similar to the one Dominic and Carrie-Anne were in, with the large living room on the lower floor.

Kirsten stared into the darkness. Her eyes were used to it now and she could see no one. Quietly, she made her way over to a small office area, again finding no one, and then walked delicately to the stairs that led to the upper floor. She crept up, one at a time, aware that at any moment, someone could appear within the cabin.

As she reached the top, she saw the landing that led to the

three rooms upstairs. She crouched for a moment, listening into the dark. The left-hand side would be the master bedroom with an en suite. There would be a separate toilet just ahead, and to the right, there would be another smaller bedroom. Kirsten walked forward, aiming to go to the bedroom initially but then she heard the flush of the toilet.

Kirsten made her way quickly to the right into the smaller bedroom and once there, ducked down and rolled underneath the bed. It was only just after she did so, that a light came on and she found herself stuck. Whoever it was, sat down on the bed and remained there for the next hour.

Kirsten slowly stretched herself, trying to keep her muscles moving. This was the help for the night, the one who was protecting Hutchinson's cabin, making sure no one came in. Kirsten was pretty sure that she could come out and surprise him but then Hutchinson would know somebody had been in and so she decided to remain in position. It was another hour after that before she heard on her earpiece. 'Kilo, he's on the move back. I'll tail and make sure he goes there but it looks like he's in for the night. The woman is with him as well.'

Kirsten didn't know whether to curse or be happy; at least she'd be on the move soon. Five minutes later, she heard the door downstairs open and the person on the bed jumped up, walked quickly out of the room, and switched off the light. There was a brief handover downstairs where voices made sure that everything was okay before she heard the front door open and close again.

Kirsten rolled out from under the bed and took up a position at the door. The light came on in the landing. Then she heard someone making their way up. The footsteps were light, more delicate than a man's. She reckoned whoever it was, was with him and turning in for the night. Kirsten remained in her position and five minutes later Hutchison came upstairs as well. The lights were put out in the rest of the cabin. When she looked out from her position, she could see a light eking out under the door of the main bedroom.

'Kilo, this is Delta. Returned back to base and you're not here. Where are you? Advise.'

Kirsten began to tap Morse code onto her mic. She knew she was in a place where she could do this, but she'd rather not speak. When she had finished passing her message, Dominic replied, 'Delta understood. Advise if diversion is necessary.'

Dominic wasn't looking for the answer now, but Kirsten realised he'd stay awake along with Carrie-Anne to run the diversion if necessary to let her get out of the room. Kirsten spent the next hour listening to what was going on inside the bedroom. As she did so, she thought about the fact that she hadn't been involved in any of these sorts of bedroom activities in a while now. The likelihood of them would be less, given how much the job was taking her away from everyone. But she was on task at the moment, and she couldn't let these things come in to her mind, for they would distract at critical moments.

The light in the bedroom went out, the two partners seemingly satisfied, and then after another ten minutes, Kirsten could hear snoring. She made her way down the stairs again before making her way to the office suite. There was a locked drawer, so Kirsten took out her lock-picking tools, spent thirty seconds working, and opened the drawers without even thinking about it.

She carefully scanned through papers that were there. There was significant information about what Hutchinson was up to, including notes and figures which in the hands of Justin Chivers could no doubt lead to various company fronts that Hutchinson had. Unfortunately, Kirsten had to leave everything behind. She took out her camera and started photographing some of them, but she realised none of them related to what she really wanted. Kirsten continued her search and started rifling through his pockets. In the suit jacket was a leather wallet with an H motif. When she picked up the wallet, she took out every one of his cards and any other paraphernalia that was inside. There was one small note, scrunched up inside, with two words on it. Mr. MacIver.

Why keep a note like this? thought Kirsten. *It's so simple and scrunched up. It means nothing to no one. If somebody found this, what could they deduce from it? Unless they knew something about what Hutchinson was up to.*

Kirsten scoured the rest of the cabin, but she found little of use, so she made her way out to the balcony, closing the door before lifting herself up onto the side of the ship. She crawled across, noting that a few more of the cabin lights were on inside but no one was out on their balcony probably due to the light rain that was starting to fall. *Blessed be the rain,* thought Kirsten, for by keeping the balconies clear she was able to get back in no time at all. Landing on the balcony of Dominic and Carrie-Anne's cabin, she gently rapped the door which was opened for her, and Carrie-Anne helped her inside to the sofa.

'Do you want a coffee?' asked Dominic, quietly.

'Go on then,' said Kirsten and began to take off her balaclava. Inside, she was hot but in truth, the night had gone easily and there had been no cause for violence. No one had seen her, and she'd been able to complete a full search. She believed no one knew she had been there.

'You find anything,' asked Carrie-Anne, sitting opposite her boss.

'I've got some documents and records that Justin is going to be interested in but with regards to what we're doing, I'm not sure. There was a scrunched-up piece of notepaper stuck inside his wallet. One of those things that people keep because they need to.'

'Anything on it?' asked Dom, handing his boss a coffee. 'There's a name,' said Kirsten, 'Mr. MacIver.'

'MacIver, is that it?'

'Exactly, only the two words.'

'Did you find anything else?'

'No. Nothing so far. I didn't get into his bedroom. That's the only place I didn't get. He was far too busy in there tonight.'

'Oh, aye,' said Dominic, 'was it a listening watch, then?'

'Unfortunately,' said Kirsten.

'Are you wanting to crash here for the night?' said Dom. 'If you're feeling tired, you can get some sleep. I'll run cover for you here.'

'No,' said Kirsten. 'I need to be out and about, be seen at least so I'm going to make my way back downstairs back to my own cabin. Then I'll go out for an hour or so and then put myself away for the evening. Before I do, give us your phone. Let's get hold of Justin.'

'This is Justin looking to go to bed,' said a voice on the end.

'You work whenever I tell you to work,' said Kirsten. 'Listen up. MacIver, Mr. MacIver. Have we got anybody on ship of that name, crew, or passenger?'

'Just give me a minute,' said Justin, and Kirsten swore she could hear the fingers tapping away on the keyboard.

'I've got a couple of MacIvers. There's three Mrs. MacIvers. Nothing flagging up about them at the moment.'

'Give me the rundown about them. Fire it through to my inbox and I'll look at it on my phone,' said Kirsten. 'It might not have anything to do with this case, but we'll need to check it out.' Kirsten looked up at Dominic. 'That means in the morning, Dominic, Carrie-Anne, and you are going to find who these people are.'

'Yes, boss.'

With that, Kirsten closed down the phone call with Justin, barely giving a thank you. She took off her black garb, stuffed it into her rucksack, and then slung that over her shoulder after putting on a pair of jeans and a t-shirt. 'Have a good night,' she said to Dominic and Carrie-Anne.

'Oh, we will do, the guest bed is very comfortable.'

Kirsten laughed but made her way out of the front door, checking to make sure no one was in the corridor before she left and then made her way down to her own cabin. Opening it, she realised that she quite fancied the idea of a living room and an upstairs in her suite, as opposed to the bed and table, the small desk, and then the tiny balcony on the outside.

She was, however, eight decks below where the salubrious cabins were. Kirsten stepped back out of the cabin half an hour later and took a walk around the ship. She stopped into one of the bars for half an hour, talking to the barman and some man named Daniel who bored her silly with his talk of how the great industrialisation of the West led to the demise of every other part of the globe. Quite what he was doing here, Kirsten was unsure of, but he certainly didn't have that holiday feel. It was two in the morning when Kirsten made her way back into her cabin, falling down asleep after making sure everywhere was locked up.

I need a good one sleep, she thought and almost instantly her eyes closed.

Chapter 16

Kirsten was lying on the beach. This came as a little bit of a shock to her because the last she'd known, she was on a cruise ship. There was a wind blowing which there had been on the boat as well but this wind was racing over her tummy. It was warm, the sort of breeze you could stand in all day. Above her, she saw wispy palm leaves gently moving back and forward. Beside her was a large tumbler, full of some sort of yellow liquid and adorned with bits of fruit at the top.

In the distance, she could hear a steel drum band, and just off to the side, she was aware of somebody coming up the beach. Looking down at her body, she was somewhat shocked at the bikini she was wearing because it really was not her. Swimwear was for practical reasons, for moving quickly through the water. What she was wearing at the moment may have been for practical reasons as well but possibly the practicalities of catching a partner. The sun was glaring towards her, and she had to shield her eyes when she turned to look at who was marching up along the sand.

It was a definitely a male figure, but she couldn't see his face due to the sun and when he flopped down beside her, she still had no notion of who it was. She reached over, touching him on the shoulder, looking to see his face and he rolled towards her as she rolled to him, both of them finding the edge of their loungers at the same time. Together, they tipped over and landed in the sand almost on top of each other. Her eyes saw the face of her driver from London.

'What are you doing here?' she said in the sort of fashion that could only be asked in a dream.

'You must have brought me here.'

Kirsten reached out with her hand, taking the man's shoulder and pulling him close. *That must be it*, she thought.

Something was blaring, interrupting her wonder of the moment. It sounded like an air-raid siren or some sort of distress on a ship. *The ship*, she thought. Kirsten suddenly woke up.

The phone beside her bed was ringing. It wasn't the mobile, but the ship's internal phone system. A light on the phone's panel was going off as well, giving the impression of a small siren.

She picked up the phone. 'Hello?'

'Is that a Miss Kirsten Stewart?' said a rather serious voice.

'Who's asking,' said Kirsten.

'The captain is; he's requested your attendance within the next few minutes. A matter of urgency he says, ma'am. This is the first officer.'

'Thank you,' said Kirsten. Nobody else on board apart from Dominic and Carrie-Anne knew her name, so it had been given to the master of the vessel presumably. Kirsten was always wary that whatever you do, someone manages to leak who you are. Even the sincere ones get caught out.

She rolled out of bed, threw off the long t-shirt that she

was wearing, and searched inside her cupboard for some underwear. For a moment, she thought about dressing to meet the captain but given that she was being brought up for some matter that needed attending to, she slipped on her jeans, t-shirt, put the hiking boots on again, and made her way out of the cabin. It was only then she clocked that it was five in the morning.

Kirsten made her way up through the decks, taking the lift. Her hands tried to pull out her hair, fashioning it into some sort of shape until she gave up and simply tied it up in a ponytail behind her. Part of her wondered if Carrie-Anne was any good with a brush on other people's hair. As her boss, of course, she could order her to do it.

Buoyed by this fact, Kirsten arrived at the top deck and made her way to the bridge of the ship. As she knocked on the door marked Private, it was opened and a man with a lot of gold on his epaulets advised her to follow him. He said nothing but instead, Kirsten was led to a place called the Captain's Day Room and asked if she required any coffee.

Five in the morning; Kirsten certainly required coffee. She answered in the affirmative and took a seat. Two minutes later, a rather serious gentleman entered.

'Good morning, ma'am. I take it you've been woken from your sleep as abruptly as I was.'

'Very much so, captain. As I'm speaking to the master of the vessel, I assume this is quite serious.'

'I'm not sure who I'm speaking to,' he said. 'However, I did speak to a woman called Hunt who advised me that I was to defer to you with regards to our situation.'

'Well, I'd say I'm more here for advice,' said Kirsten. 'You are the master of the ship. Thereby, by law, you have to make the decisions, so by all means, you'll get the benefit of my wisdom and experience, but I won't be in charge of you, sir.'

This seemed to buoy the captain somewhat, and he sat down momentarily while the coffees arrived. However, once the steward had left, the captain picked his coffee up, stood, and began to pace the room.

'The ship has received a threat, not directly but through your people or at least through London, as they said.'

'Be specific, please,' said Kirsten. 'When you were speaking to Miss Hunt, what did she say to you, exactly?'

'She said to me that the vessel was under threat. London had been advised and that a certain party would be willing to destroy the vessel if we did not find an item onboard, an item that you're aware of, I believe,' said the captain.

'That's why I'm on board. I'm in the process of looking for it. Did she say anything else?'

'She said people had put a timeline on finding the item and said it had to be found before our stop in Stornoway; otherwise, this ship would be destroyed. They also advised that if any deviation on the ship's normal course was taken, then they would trigger an explosion because they believe that the item would be taken that way. They were also not happy with our landing in Shetland, and I've been advised that we should not disembark there.'

'Now, if they know it's here and they think somebody here has it, then by keeping it on board, they think they're doing us a favour,' said Kirsten. 'However, what it does do is put your ship, your crew, and your people at great risk.' Kirsten sipped her coffee, thinking for a moment, but the master continued to walk up and down.

'If I have to keep this quiet,' he said, 'what do I do? How do I not stop in Shetland? The weather's going to be okay. It's not like I can cancel it on weather grounds.'

'What would keep everybody away from us?' asked Kirsten. 'What possible reason could you have as a master for keeping everyone else off your vessel?'

'We could declare an infection of some sort. We wouldn't be allowed to land anywhere on that basis. We could still steam about, follow our route, say we were just continuing with the passage until our doctor decided that everything was okay. That would buy us time.'

'When do we plan to be in Stornoway?' asked Kirsten.

'Two days,' said the man, 'we've got two days to solve this. Otherwise, I may have to start taking everybody off the vessel.'

'If it comes to that,' said Kirsten, 'we'll need to do it quietly. We'll need to work out how because the moment they see anyone leave, they will destroy the vessel. If I can make you aware, sir, that the item they're looking for, as I understand it, is believed to be of high value to a certain country. I believe the country would probably want that item to fall to the sea rather than to fall into the hands of a rival country. So basically, I'm saying to you that we've got to find it or this vessel—and everybody on it—is as good as gone.'

'So, what am I to do for those two days?' asked the master.

'Number one,' said Kirsten, 'you don't invite me up here again, it's too public, you know? Yes. A friend of a friend knows us, but beyond that, you don't invite me up. As you can see, I'm dressed here as one of your less prominent passengers. I'm meant to be unknown. I have other people here as well and we will find the item for you. We will secure it and when we do, you'll advise London, then everything will calm down. There may also be people watching here. When we go about our business, we'll be as discreet as possible,' said Kirsten, 'but unfortunately, things may come to head at times, and you'll have to run cover for that. Everything has to continue as normal, at least until we get towards Stornoway. I'll get one of my other people to make contact, somebody who could do with a tour of the vessel as well. They'll start planning with you how we get everybody off this ship if things don't go well.'

'I would suggest you make them go well,' said the master; 'the vessel isn't called *Her Majesty's Pride* for no reason. We are the biggest passenger ship in the world. The biggest cruise ship, the pride of the UK launched by her Majesty's own fair hand. If this vessel were to suffer, then it would reflect badly on the UK. It would reflect badly on us all.'

'If this vessel suffers,' said Kirsten, 'we won't be worried about how it's reflecting. The people we're talking about will destroy it in such a way that neither you or I will ever make our pension. When my colleague comes up, you need to have a chat about where would be the best place to plant explosives to sink this vessel. They'll be well hidden, hard to find. We may need to get a number of your crew, well trusted, who can go and look, but not do anything with them when you find them.'

'Do you have any idea who's doing this?' said the master.

Kirsten wanted to say, *No, we have no idea. We're running in the dark and all we have is a scrap of paper with a name on it,* but she didn't.

'We're on it and we've got it covered,' said Kirsten. 'Do you know anybody by the name of MacIver on board? Any of your crew?'

'Well, I can't know everybody on the crew, but there's none among the senior staff. I don't know any MacIvers. I could contact the rest of the staff, find out for you.'

'No, you don't do anything. I have other ways and means. The rest of you are to carry on as normal, continue to host your dinners, continue to run the ship as if it's being exercised, ready for sea. That's very important.

'As you wish. Will you keep me informed about developments?'

'No,' said Kirsten, 'I'll talk to you if I need you. I'll talk to you if we have to get things done. I will send my colleague to talk to you about how we get everybody off this ship if we have to run. Outside of that, no, I won't talk to you.'

The captain turned and made his way over to the side of the room where a coffee pot had been left. He poured himself some more before turning back to Kirsten. 'Would you like some more?'

Kirsten shook her head. 'I've got about forty-eight hours at most to solve this,' she said. 'Time to get cracking but thank you for the coffee.'

As Kirsten stood up and went to leave, the man reached across and took her by the arm. 'Just promise me one thing. You give the people in here a fighting chance. Don't just leg it at the end, leaving them all to die.'

Kirsten wondered what it was about her that gave her the appearance of someone who would just cut and run because nobody when she was a police officer, would ever have questioned whether or not she was going to give people a chance to live.

'Of course, I will, and we'll be here helping you evacuate them if we have to. Until then, carry on as normal, and don't tell anybody else about this.' Before she left, Kirsten had a thought. 'Can your doctor be trusted?' she asked.

'I think so. Oxford man, former officer.'

'Can you bring him in?' asked Kirsten, 'When you do, I want you to brief him on exactly what's going to happen.'

'Okay,' said the captain, 'and you're going to do what?'

'Watch him,' said Kirsten, 'watch him and decide.'

'Decide what?' asked the captain.

'Whether or not he's coming down with an illness as well.'

It was twenty minutes later when a rather haggard doctor walked in. It seemed he'd been up last night until about two in the morning as well, entertaining certain people, and right now, the last thing he wanted to do was any sort of work. Kirsten sat in the corner while the man was briefed about what was going to happen and told that once they'd left Orkney, he was to make sure that he declared an illness that was going to restrict anyone from coming off the vessel. The doctor kept looking over at Kirsten, but he answered every question direct to the captain. At the end of the conversation, the captain asked him if he had any questions.

'Just the one? Who's she?'

'This is a friend of ours, she's helping advise me.'

'Then she'll need to advise me as well. I'm the medical officer here. You're asking me to declare something that truly isn't right. What's going on?'

Kirsten stood up, walked over to the man, standing in front of him so he had to look up at her.

'The captain tells me you're ex-military. I'm one of those people that you don't ask who they are. I'm one of those people you never see. And I'm one of those people who if you don't go along with this, who's going to have to deal with you in some sort of fashion.'

Kirsten was convinced of the doctor and left the room after

advising the captain that, once again, he should just get on with it. She made her own room at six o'clock and thought about calling her troops together, but instead, as they'd been out the night before, she was going to give them an hour's rest. Another part of her asked, *Why? You're up. You've got forty-eight hours; why shouldn't they get going too?* With that, she picked up the internal phone to call Dominic.

Chapter 17

Kirsten Stewart slipped inside the door of Dominic's suite and made her way over to the cafetière, pouring out some of the pre-packaged coffee and then checking the kettle to see if it was warm. Having found it wasn't, she pressed down on the switch and turned to see Carrie-Anne making her way down from the upper floor. She was wearing a short dressing gown, and Kirsten looked at her a little bit amused.

'Well, I was going to pop out on deck, bring Dom his breakfast. We spun some story last night about not being married that long. Kind of have to keep up the image, don't we?' Carrie-Anne smiled and gave a wink to Kirsten, but she really had no time for this today.

'That's all well and good, but things have changed, and we need to move quickly.'

'How do you mean?' asked Dom, entering from the balcony, looking worried and pulling a chair aside before sitting down in it.

'You'd better grab a seat as well,' Kirsten said to Carrie-Anne, and the Welsh woman plonked herself on the edge of a sideboard. 'It appears that our friendly country who simply wants to get their diamond back is becoming rather unfriendly, to the tune that if we don't have the diamond back to them by the time we hit Stornoway, they're going to do something to this vessel. Something catastrophic. London felt it was essential to get hold of the captain and then to contact myself.'

'So, what's the captain say about it?' asked Dom.

'He's been rather good actually,' said Kirsten. 'Has taken the advice that I've issued.'

'What's that?'

'Well, he should carry on as normal. He's going to give us time, because having found the name of MacIver in the wallet of Hutchinson, we have a task to get to. The captain, however, needs to make sure things continue. He will declare that the ship is having an outbreak at this time, and therefore we won't be landing up in Shetland. We weren't due to land on Orkney anyway, but this will keep everything on the boat. No one can get off yet.'

'Not unless somebody brings a boat alongside and they jump,' said Carrie-Anne.

'That's a good one to cover. We'll need somebody on the outside then when we get close to Orkney. Carrie-Anne, that's your job.'

The woman raised her hand to her hair, and Kirsten thought she was going to ask if she could've a better job due to the detrimental damage from excessive wind, but she simply seemed to be yawning slightly.

'I'm sorry,' said Kirsten. 'Was it a rough night last night?'

'We did double watch,' she said. 'Went out, strolling around, see what we could find, but we got nothing. I'm not long back in.'

'Well, we've no time to rest,' said Kirsten. Grabbing Dom's

tablet, she looked up his contact for Justin, before placing the tablet on a desk. Soon, Justin's face was looking back at them. He gave a rather overt look at Carrie-Anne's dressing gown, something which Kirsten thought unnecessary, but she suspected he had his cover to keep up. Not that Carrie-Anne seemed to mind the attention anyway.

'Justin, you're on passenger records. Crew as well. See if you can find anything out for us. We know there's a certain number of MacIvers, we're going to check them now. But check up their lives off the vessel—where they've come from, what they've done. I'm also going to search the dead areas of the vessel, so to speak. Where they keep the bodies when people die on board. I'm sure there's not anything untoward down there at the moment, but it's worth a check. Have we got anything since last night?' Kirsten asked Justin, 'because at the moment it seems pretty thin, and given we've got forty-eight hours to turn this thing around, I'm not in a very happy place.'

'Got a faint link,' said Justin. 'One of the crew has ties to Hutchinson. She works in the galley. Reasonably high up, something like third chef. Her name is Susannah Small, but from the description I've got of her, she's not that tiny. Apparently, she's got blonde hair, probably close to the height of Carrie-Anne, and likes jogging and lacrosse. That's just little bits I've picked up from the crew profile or their own personnel files. She's been on for quite a while though, from the start of this endeavour with this vessel.'

'What do you want to do with her?' asked Dom. 'We get the captain to bring her up to his top-level, have a bit of a conversation up there?'

'No,' said Kirsten. 'She's got a link to Hutchinson. At the moment, we haven't heard anything from him. We've got the name MacIver, that's it, no idea what that means. Hutchinson's clearly ahead of us. We've got forty-eight hours, Hutchinson's got to be thinking he's got to make a move as well soon. Let's see what develops between the two of them. We'll keep an eye on her for the next twelve hours. If nothing develops, then we'll intervene.'

'You could find out what sort of shifts she's on,' said Carrie-Anne. 'Easier to trace her that way. It will be best if one of us isn't seen all the time with her.'

'Good idea. Dom, you check the dead lockup. Carrie-Anne, you keep an eye on Hutchinson, I'll keep an eye on our Susannah Small, see what comes of it today. Dom, when you've checked the dead area, get onto the MacIvers on the vessel, see what comes of that.'

Kirsten finished her coffee, leaving Justin to get on with his duties and then made her way out, pretending to roam the ship in search of interest, but she made her way down towards the galley. When she arrived, she found a porter close by and asked him if he knew when Susannah Small was coming on. The man looked at her strangely.

'Oh, it's just a friend of my daughter is friends with Susannah and asked if I could pass something along. It's probably best if I do it in person. Do you know when she's about?'

'Well, she won't be on for a while,' he said, 'I believe she's on later this morning and then she'll be off tonight.'

'Okay,' said Kirsten. 'Maybe I'll try and find her in her cabin. Do you know where that is?'

'Passengers are not allowed inside those areas. Maybe I can go and get her for you.'

'Oh, don't be daft. I don't want to take you away from your work,' said Kirsten, 'Tell you what? Tell me roughly which deck it is and I'll hang about outside. I'm sure I'll be able to find her. She's quite easy to notice, I think. Tall and leggy with the blonde hair.'

Kirsten watched the man's face as he smiled, nodding. 'That's her. But if you're not sure, ma'am, I could go and get her.'

'No, it's fine. Which deck is it?'

'She'll be down on deck five, it's the crew quarters down there, but you're not allowed on that one, so you'll see her exit round about deck six.'

Kirsten nodded and then made her way off towards deck six. Arriving there, she saw the coded door that let the crew in to descend down to their quarters beneath. Standing around casually, she watched three people come and punch in a code. From the first, she got the third digit. From the second, the first two. From the third one, she got digits four and five. Tapping them in, Kirsten made her way down, deeper into the belly of the ship. As she walked along, someone gave her a look.

She simply stared back at them, marching along confidently, striding to wherever. She didn't know wherever was, but this was not the person to ask. Instead, after she turned right at three corners, she pulled a young man aside asking him if he knew Susannah Small.

'Susannah? She's gone up that flight of stairs. I think she's heading up to the pool.'

'I didn't think we were allowed in the pool,' said Kirsten.

'Well, the captain's okayed it at the moment for certain staff. Not that many people on board are allowed to go and be recreational during certain hours. You should check your sheets.'

'I will do, I love the pool,' said Kirsten, and turned right and marched away. When she didn't hear any noises from behind her, she believed she'd gotten away with her deception.

Taking a detour back to her room, Kirsten picked up her swimsuit and then made her way up towards the pools on the upper deck. She walked beside the water, scanning for a tall blonde woman, and then spotted one on the far side of the pool. Quickly, Kirsten made her way inside one of the cubicles, changed, and came out to find the woman still lying there, so Kirsten stepped inside the pool and began swimming up and down.

She always thought it was better to be engaged in some sort of activity, rather than simply to watch. As she continued up and down, she spotted Carrie-Anne striding along the side of the pool in her bikini before laying a towel and lying down on a lounger. Twenty seconds later at the opposite side of the pool, Hutchinson emerged from the men's changing rooms. Kirsten saw Carrie-Anne's face, watching him all the way along until he sat down on the lounger beside Susannah Small.

Kirsten continued to swim, but her eye was kept on Susannah and Hutchinson. They seemed to be freely engaging with each other. At one point, Hutchinson stood up, went over behind the lounger of Susannah Small, putting both of his hands on her shoulders, probably in a more than therapeutic way. Hutchinson then indicated the Jacuzzi at the side of the pool, and the pair of them made their way over.

Kirsten was quite surprised when once in the Jacuzzi, the man pulled Susannah Small over, making her sit on his knee, his arms wrapped around her. This was as far as the activity went. Kirsten thought it more as romantic, rather than inappropriate, but she did think this was all very sudden. Maybe it was just the way Susannah did business. Kirsten had heard about women like that, who preferred to keep men they met dangling. Overpower them with their sexuality, rather than simply trusting their face. Kirsten was never one who could do that, but she swore Carrie-Anne could pull it off. Kirsten continued up and down until she realised that the hour was getting close to eleven.

Hutchinson and Susannah Small went in and out of the Jacuzzi several times, but he now seemed to be bidding her farewell. Kirsten made her way out to the changing rooms, drying quickly, before following Susannah Small down to deck five, where she entered her cabin and Kirsten walked straight past. Loitering around the corridors wasn't easy, but she managed to pick up Susannah Small's trail again, but this time, the woman was dressed in chef's whites. First, she contacted Carrie-Anne, who explained Hutchinson had gone back to his cabin. When Susannah Small presented herself in the kitchen for her shift, Kirsten made her own way back to her cabin and took a shower, trying to think through what had happened. Susannah would be off again that night. Should Kirsten move quickly or should she leave her to see what she did that evening? Would she go back to Hutchinson? Kirsten would want to get close to pick up that conversation.

When Kirsten stepped out of the shower and dried herself down, she wrapped herself up in one of the white gowns from the ship and stepped out into her small cabin. Dom was sitting down inside, helping himself to a cup of coffee.

'Apologies, but I couldn't really hang outside and wait for you to open the door.'

'It's fine,' she said, sitting down on the bed close by him. 'What have you found out?'

'Well, there's nobody dead down below. The dead lockup's

got nobody in it and I had a hunt around for the MacIvers. Three women on board, but none of them so far have been out and about much. One went down for her lunch. Another one was accompanied by Spanish gentlemen on a tour of the vessel and then back into their cabin, and the last one spent the morning playing two hours of croquet. Rather spiffing, really.'

'So far, that's a dead end. We need to pull them in as well, but I'd rather see what develops first,' said Kirsten, rubbing a towel through her hair. 'Susannah Small's off from working this evening. I'm going to trail her again. Carrie-Anne can cover off Hutchinson. Do you think we should watch the MacIvers this evening?'

'Well, I can do that if you wish,' said Dom. 'Carrie-Anne's got enough to look after Hutchinson, and she's got the skill and the flair to attract his attention, if needed. I doubt he's going to want to talk to a small bald-headed man like myself.'

Kirsten shook her head laughing. 'The man certainly seems to have his head turned by women. It's not a bad thing if Hutchinson can be turned that way. We could use that later on, if needs be. Okay,' said Kirsten, 'we do that tonight then. I'll pick up Susannah Small, see where she's going. Carrie-Anne sticks on Hutchinson, and you take on the MacIvers. We'll see if Justin can come up with something as well.'

'So far, it's been very quiet from onshore, and that bothers me.'

'Justin's good at what he does, Dom. If he's not finding stuff, it's not there.'

'Have you seen anything of an Arab gentleman?' asked Dom.

'Not on my travels. There no doubt might be some on board, but if he's got the diamond, he's moving it in a rather quiet fashion. Otherwise, Hutchinson would be walking around here looking for Arab gentlemen. It'd be a crude way to get on to things, but it might just work.'

'Maybe it's something we should think about closer to the time.'

'Agreed,' said Kirsten. 'If push comes to shove and we find nothing, we start hauling the Arab gentlemen in as well. All of them, whoever they are. We'll probably get done for racism, but if it will stop something happening to this ship. I'll take that.'

Dom grinned. 'Yes. That'll be the thing, won't it? Stop the ship from going down, but you could send down yourself, because you had to pull in some foreign people to do it.'

'Right, well, you get on,' Kirsten said to Dom, 'I'm going to get changed here, and this cabin's far too cramped for you to be joining me.'

'Thank your lucky stars it's not Justin with you,' said Dom, walking out of the cabin and shutting the door carefully behind him.

Justin really has them played well, doesn't he? she thought. *None of them suspect. None of them have clocked it.* Then she thought about how she had discovered his secret. It hadn't been easy, and all she'd been left with was an admiration for a man pretending to be a flirt, when he would be happier looking at the other man in the room.

Chapter 18

Kirsten was keeping her casual look up that night when she headed out in her jeans and T-shirt. She had arrived out too early but made a careful surveillance of the restaurants before then popping through to the back to see the chefs at work. She realised that Susannah Small was still working. When she clocked off around eight o'clock, Kirsten loitered not far from the door where most of the crew seemed to enter into the passenger areas. Not that many were about but those who were had obviously been given the privilege by the captain. They seemed to always come through one of three different doors. This meant Kirsten was able to pick up Susannah Small quite easily and she was quite taken aback as the woman made her way along the vessel. She wore a skirt that Kirsten thought was far too short for her, one that Kirsten certainly wouldn't wear, high-heeled shoes, and a rather smart top. Her hair had been brushed and she had taken a shower to take care of the grease from working in the kitchen.

As Kirsten followed her, keeping a discreet distance, she found Susannah making her way to the higher decks before cutting through to the cabin suites Kirsten was familiar with. Kirsten walked past as Hutchinson opened his door, smelling of strong cologne, and invited the woman in. As Kirsten turned the corner, she almost bumped into Carrie-Anne.

'Both inside the same place. I need to get in there,' said Kirsten.

'Maybe you could climb your way over again,' suggested Carrie-Anne, but Kirsten made her way back around the corner and checked the corridor again before walking on round.

'Did you notice something?' she asked Carrie-Anne when she met her again.

'Faces, new faces,' said Carrie-Anne.

'Exactly. Having watched this place for a day, I've started to notice Hutchinson's men, but some of them aren't. Let's just keep on the move.'

Kirsten spent the next ten minutes walking up and down corridors, poking her head around corners, to see the same faces loitering close to Hutchinson's cabin. Kirsten checked her weapon and suggested Carrie-Anne do the same. When she looked out over the corridor again, Kirsten could see the same men performing what amounted to a patrol in front of Hutchinson's cabin. Kirsten kept herself hidden as best as she could.

'Do you think they're going for her?' asked Carrie-Anne.

'Almost certainly,' said Kirsten, and tapped her microphone. 'Delta, Delta, this is Kilo. Kilo, require assistance immediately outside Hutchinson's cabin. Come in.'

'This is Delta; Roger.'

Carrie-Anne was dressed in high heels and a dress that looked like she was off to dinner, but despite this, the woman seemed to move eloquently in them. Kirsten, with her hiking boots and jeans on, felt comfortable. She slipped down to the corridor quickly, walking down behind one of the men before slipping into another passageway before he turned around again. She was now only fifteen feet from Hutchinson's cabin but she didn't need to be that close to hear the loud thump.

A door crashed open and Hutchison gave a cry from inside. There wasn't gunfire, but rather the discharge of a silenced weapon, and Kirsten made her way quickly towards Hutchison's cabin. As she rounded the corner, the man drew his weapon, but Kirsten tagged him first to the head and then to the heart before continuing her run. When she reached the cabin door, she saw a gun pointed out of it, and moved herself back out of the way. She heard footsteps coming to the door.

Kirsten kicked it hard and managed to clatter it into an on-coming gunman. Kirsten followed in to sustain her advantage. The man was stumbling backwards, but his weapon was still loose and swinging, so Kirsten took his hand and slammed it against the side of the cabin. As she did so, a figure in a red dress slipped past her, high heels on, and performed a kick into the ribs of another man in front of her. Carrie-Anne's blonde hair could be seen swinging wildly as she then performed a punch to the face of the man in front of her.

Kirsten saw a man holding Hutchison outside on the deck. He already had his hands on Hutchison's backside and was pulling him up, ready to tip him over the safety barrier into the water. Kirsten fired twice. The man fell to the ground on the balcony and Hutchison slid back to the floor.

The fight wasn't over yet, and Kirsten swept to the stairs. Making her way up, she saw a face appear at the top and she fired before it quickly disappeared back. Kirsten had two choices. She could retreat, or she could get up there quickly and try and follow home any advantage she had, and it was this urgency that drove her on.

As she turned onto the landing, she saw the muzzle of the weapon pointing out and slammed it against the wall. A man threw a punch, catching her on the chin, but Kirsten shook it off, driving her shoulder up and into him, all the time keeping his hand and the gun in it pressed tight to the wall. She kneed him several times before grabbing the top of his head and then driving a knee up into his face. The man fell cold to the floor.

As another face appeared at the bedroom beyond, Kirsten heard a silenced shot over the top of her head, and the man fell to the ground. Kirsten kicked open the bedroom door and found Susannah Small lying on the bed, shaking.

'Bathroom's clear,' shouted Carrie-Anne. A moment later, 'Small bedroom clear.'

'Check front door. Isolate. When Delta's here, tell him to protect. Get the man that was in the corridor back inside before anybody sees him. I'm going to try and go dark on this.'

As every cabin wasn't occupied, Kirsten thought they had a chance, due to the silenced weapons, of actually keeping this quiet. Several of the men had been downed and wouldn't be getting back up again, but Kirsten was going to have to discreetly put them somewhere in the meantime. As she saw Carrie-Anne go to the front door, Kirsten made her way out to the balcony where Hutchison was lying down, his face beaten. Kirsten saw Dom arrive at the front door and shouted over her shoulder at him to clean up the mess in the hall and then told Carrie-Anne to take care of Susannah up top.

'He almost had me over. He almost had me over,' said Hutchison, seemingly not able to comprehend what had happened.

'And he would've done if I hadn't taken him down,' said

Kirsten, 'so you start talking.'

'What do you mean start talking?'

'You know what I mean. You're here for a reason. They're here for a reason. They think that you know something. Either that or you have what I want in here.'

'I don't have the diamond. I've come to get the diamond. Look. Go in. Look underneath there. There are three cases. There's serious money in there. There's over a couple of million.'

Kirsten was going to make her way inside to check, but she doubted Hutchinson was lying. 'So where is it? Why is Susannah Small upstairs? Why have you been meeting her?'

'She's my eyes on the ship,' said Hutchinson. 'I had a fling with her a while ago, then I remembered she was getting this job. We knew the diamonds were coming here. We knew they were coming on board, so I asked her to keep a lookout for me. But I couldn't just go swanning around. That's why she's come discreetly.'

'Not that discreetly,' said Kirsten. 'I've got bodies here. This is going to be a mess to clean up.'

'But you haven't found out much, have you?' asked Hutchinson.

'No. We still want it. Who are these people, anyway?'

'They showed up before. I think they're Belgian—Furrer's men by the look of it. You know what he's like. Wants everything. Had that tussle down in Strathpeffer. We nearly got it there. Do you know that? We almost got it.'

'How did you know it was going to be on board?' asked Kirsten.

'Just a guess.'

Dom came racing inside. 'We've got a problem. We've still

got four men outside watching here.'

'Watching with what intent?' asked Kirsten.

'I think they're coming for him,' said Dom. 'Now we need to move him and quick. We also need to move the girl above. But where are we going to take them?'

'We can't take them to yours,' Kirsten said to Dom. 'It's not safe. We take him down below. You said there was no one in the dead room, didn't you?' Dom nodded. 'Well, that's the place then. We can stick them in there for a while. I need to talk to the captain.'

'The captain?' said Hutchinson. 'But you're not. Who the hell are you?'

'You'll find out soon enough. Now shut up,' said Kirsten. She looked at Dom and saw Carrie-Anne bringing Susannah Small down at gunpoint. 'We'll also need to cover up what's happening with her,' said Dom.

'How close are they outside?' asked Kirsten.

'They've got eyes on the front door. It's not going to be easy to get out.'

She turned to Hutchinson looking at her. 'Is there anyone in the cabin next door?'

'Not that I'm aware of.'

'Okay, then,' said Kirsten. 'That's where we go from. Firstly, you, shut it. I'm going to take you somewhere safe because if I leave you here, you're a dead man. You're not in your territory now, Hutchinson. You've picked off more than you can chew.'

She stood up and looked over the panelling that separated one balcony from the next. Four balconies along, someone was in, and she realised it would be another five in the other direction to get into Dom and Carrie-Anne's balcony.

'Want another option?' asked Dom. 'We could go up to mine

and come in from there.'

'Let's pincer them. You don't know how many are out there, do you? How many do you think?'

'Well, I counted three,' said Dom, 'but could be more.'

'Well, when we clean them up, this would be the place to hold them.'

Dom nodded. 'What do we do with these two though?'

'I think Charlie needs to babysit.' Kirsten turned round to Hutchinson. 'You're going to follow what I say, you're going to do it, and you're going to be bloody glad of me when it's all over. This man here is going to take you over several of these barriers onto a balcony. He's going to take you inside a room there where my other friend is going to look after you. You're going to say nothing and she's going to tie you up. Once we have everything clear, we're going to put you somewhere else and then you're going to answer some questions for me. Do you understand?'

'Aye,' said Hutchinson. 'Just get those bastards off my back.'

'Right. Delta, get on the move. Charlie,' she called over at Carrie-Anne. 'With Delta, back to yours, then you babysit. Delta is going to clean the corridors with me.' Carrie-Anne nodded and hauled Susannah Small over towards Hutchinson.

'Sorry to bother you, ma'am,' said Kirsten. 'Go over there and do everything this woman tells you. Okay, time to move, guys.'

Kirsten leaped over the barrier beside her and made her way through into the cabin. It was a large one, identical but on the reverse side to that of Hutchinson's. Kirsten got to the door, where the spy hole allowed her to look out into the corridor. It was that same fish lens view that all doors had, and Kirsten was able to see people go past but was struggling for any sort of detail. She tapped her microphone. 'Appears we've got at least three on the move in the corridor, Delta. Tell me when ready. Pincer them and then we sweep round. I want five corridors back minimum.'

'Roger.'

Kirsten stood beside the door, watching the corridor as people went back and forward. At one point, she saw what looked like a rather drunk punter making his way along and one of the men rather roughly moved him aside, telling him to get clear. She knew they'd have to be careful.

'Delta's ready,' came the call, and Kirsten looked out, seeing someone walk past. 'Delta go; Delta go.'

Kirsten flung her door open, stepped out and struck someone across the back of the head. He fell to the ground, out cold, but along the corridor from her she saw someone spin round. Kirsten went down on one knee, drew her weapon, fired twice, and saw the man tumble. Behind her, she heard somebody else tumble. She scoured the corridor quickly up and down. There were three people lying on the floor. Two were probably dead. One was out cold.

The only other person in the corridor was Dominic. She ran to the end of the corridor before turning right, making her way along the corridors that ran parallel. She ran at speed backwards and forwards, crisscrossing with Dominic twice. It all seemed clear, nobody else about, until she turned one other corner and almost ran into a man holding a gun in his hand. Kirsten's reactions were spontaneous but from practice. Her hand flew to the man's neck, her other hand over his mouth, driving him back into the wall. She then took the hand off his throat, grabbed his wrist, and almost snapped it as she brought it down to the wall. The gun he was holding fell. Then she turned around and drove a knee up into him. Once again, she grabbed the back of his head, driving a knee up towards it, and she could hear the smash of his nose.

It hadn't been her intention to cause a bloody mess, but it was occurring. She grabbed him, dragging him back along the corridor quickly. When she arrived in the main corridor in front of Hutchinson's suite, she made for his door, opening it and dragging the man she had inside. She then raced back outside, carefully avoiding Dom, who was busy dragging one of the dead men. It took them another thirty seconds to help both of the other men inside and they locked the door.

Kirsten made for the phone, placing a call to the captain. It took two minutes for the captain to come to the phone, but when he did, Kirsten could hear the worry in his voice.

'Captain, it's your friend from this morning. Unfortunately, we've made a bit of a mess. I need you to come down to cabin—' She checked her phone to see what the cabin number was and passed it over. 'It seems things are elevating, sir, and quickly.'

Chapter 19

'Look, captain, I know it's not great but thank you for your assistance. We'll keep them down here until we do eventually dock. One of your men needs simply to bring them food as and when needed, and under no circumstances does he let them loose.'

Kirsten was in the bow of the ship trying to brief the captain after the fiasco, as he called it, that had happened many decks above. In the room, Dominic had stored several bodies from those people who had tried to attack Hutchinson, but the room now also held Hutchinson and two of the men who they had managed to knock out rather than kill. They were all tied up, gagged as well, handcuffs fixing them to parts of the room that would not move. It wasn't an ideal situation, but Kirsten was having to think on her feet. There was a surreal scene of Carrie-Anne standing in her high heels and dress, lugging corpses into body bags and then storing them at the far side of the room.

'How many of your crew know?' asked Kirsten.

'I did what you asked,' said the captain. 'Me, my first mate, second mate, and just a couple of trusted hands—otherwise, no one.'

'Keep it that way,' said Kirsten. 'Only those men who have been down here already bring any food to our prisoners and whatever they do, they don't unbind their hands.'

'I get it and don't worry. I'll put the fear of God into them so they don't. These people have caused enough trouble.'

'They have but we also have a problem in that the diamond is still out there, and the threat is still very real, captain, so if you excuse me I need to get to work on some of these people, find out what's really going on.'

When the captain departed the room, Kirsten turned her attention to the three men who were still alive. A dark-haired man, who had caked blood now across his forehead, looked up. As Kirsten bent down close to him, he spat in her face and Kirsten wiped it off before wiping it back on him.

'That's no way to behave in front of a lady,' said Kirsten. The man spoke in a language that Kirsten wasn't too sure of.

'It's Bulgarian,' said Carrie-Anne. 'Do you want me to talk to him?'

'Since when did you speak Bulgarian?' said Kirsten.

'Well, along with the French and the German, it's one of mine although it's not on the official forms. I was taking it at a night class.' Kirsten nodded and pointed to the man, advising Carrie-Anne to carry on. The man's colleague also spoke no English, or at the very least they were deciding not to employ whatever knowledge of the language they had.

'Now, I know you can speak English,' said Kirsten to Hutchinson. 'I want to know what's going on. You're not getting out of here at the moment and you're in a world of trouble, so I think a little bit of cooperation is what's required to convince me that you aren't part of this bloodbath, that somebody simply came for you.'

'Of course, somebody came for me. You were there.'

'And you're just on a happy holiday on a ship. Susannah Small, what's that all about?'

Kirsten had stowed the crew member in a cabin allowing the captain to put a guard in with her. Like the men, she was bound but Kirsten didn't fancy leaving a woman in here on her own with the men as she wasn't sure if she could handle herself. Carrie-Anne, on the other hand, Kirsten would leave with anyone.

'Susannah is just . . .'

'Well, how would you put it? A friend or contact.'

'Maybe a contact.'

'It didn't look that way in the Jacuzzi the other day.'

Hutchinson's face fell. 'Well, she's a little bit more than a contact. A good-looking woman. Someone I have been with before. When I found out the diamond was coming here onto the boat, I contacted her and yes, the ploy was to try and see what we could find. She could move about the ship easily, maybe see anything unusual. She's been into records that the captain has, crew lists, and those of passengers, trying to find out things for me about where the diamond is.'

'So, she knew it was on board?'

'No,' said Hutchinson, 'she has no idea where it is. She's been looking but she didn't know it was coming on board. I knew that.'

'Why should I believe you? Why do I not believe that she hasn't got it already, or she knows who has it?'

'Because she doesn't; it's why I didn't come with the wife. I couldn't exactly entertain Susannah if the wife was with me, could I?'

Kirsten was good at reading people, and at the moment she

felt Hutchinson wasn't lying to her. He seemed a bit out of his depth given what had happened to him and maybe he had bitten off more than he could chew.

'So, the idea was what? To come on board, see if you could find anything?'

'You found the money in my room, didn't you?'

Kirsten thought back. Dom had searched it, and he had pulled out three briefcases full of cash.

'We did. Although I'm not sure it's enough to buy what you're looking for.'

'But that's the thing,' said Hutchinson. 'I just know it's good. I know I could sell it on for a lot more. I couldn't bring much more cash on board than that. That would be a down payment because I needed to see what they were wanting, how much.'

'But you don't understand what's coming with it, do you? This diamond—' and Kirsten nearly cursed because that was all she knew about it really. It was a diamond wanted by a country. 'It's very important to some people in the Middle East. You really need to keep out of this.'

'Well, it looks like I'm out of it now, doesn't it?'

'Oh no,' said Kirsten, 'you'll be hauled into it unless you start coughing up the information. You said you knew it was on board here. How?'

Hutchinson shook his head. 'That's going to put somebody at risk if I start naming names.'

'Let me explain something,' said Kirsten, 'we're currently on board a boat that's not allowed to dock. That's not allowed to do any usual manoeuvres because a certain Middle East country is watching it. If we don't get them their diamond back within the next thirty hours or so you're going to be on board something that's liable to either go boom, sink, or get boarded. We've no idea how but they're going to take this boat out with everyone on it. At the moment, distasteful as it may be, I'm your only hope, so start telling me what happened and how you knew it was here.'

'We got wind that it went north and unlike these Arab boys, I know everyone up here. It's not all my territory, but I've got links. I called in a few favours, put the word out, and heard there was a fence in Aberdeen who had got asked to move the diamond on. Apparently, the Arab gentleman was too hot. Somebody stopped him somewhere, but he didn't have the diamond on him because he put it through other channels. He was going to rendezvous with it at some point, maybe here.'

'How do you not know where he's going to rendezvous? If you knew the fence, I take it you went and saw them?'

'Oh, I went and saw them, went and saw the family too because these people don't talk unless you give them a darn good reason. I'm sure you can appreciate that.'

Kirsten was disliking the man more and more, but she needed to keep talking to him, needed to keep the information flow going.

'So, what happened next?'

'Well, he says to me, and this is what got me, he said he won't say anything. Well, I threatened him, threatened his family. The most I got was it was heading for this ship. He said while I had targets on him, his family—other people did too. All he said to me was *Her Majesty's Pride*—three words. The man never said anything else and those words he only whispered in my ear. Always a good fence. Might use him sometime in the future for things. I guess you better be onto that lead. Following that up, hadn't you? Oh, you can't, can you? You're on the boat. Stuck here with me. Got a lot of searching to do.

You see that's what surprised me when I came on. They said this was a trial run. I didn't realise how many people were actually on board still. This thing's massive, isn't it?'

Kirsten looked at the man almost bemused. Some people had just tried to kill him. He'd been held down, tied up in the bow of a ship. Then he's being questioned and told that his life's probably going to end in the next twenty-four hours unless the person in front of him can find a certain diamond and yet the man starts talking as if he's on a holiday cruise, marvelling at everything around him.

'Don't be too hard on Susannah; she doesn't know anything. She doesn't really know much about me,' said Hutchinson. 'You can question her, but you won't get out anything more than what I've said. Yes. We've looked at records. We've dug up things around the boat, but we've found nothing. To be honest, I was getting to the point of thinking stuff this for a game of soldiers. Let's just have an enjoyable time with Susannah. She's quite the girl, isn't she?'

Again, bemused, Kirsten shook her head. Why an earth would he think Kirsten had any interest in how this woman was? Kirsten took the gag she had previously removed from the man's mouth and tied it forcefully. 'If I open this up again, you need to tell me the name of the fence. Like I said, we've got a bomb or something else that's going to do damage to the ship and take us all down. The threat's very real.'

'The man was good to me. I can't exactly open up who he was, can I?'

Kirsten put the gag back again. *Damn it*, she thought, *Why on Earth would you have this honour among thieves? Is that what it was?*

She turned around and called Carrie-Anne over. 'Who are

these people, then?'

'Working for Furrer,' said Carrie-Anne, 'professionals, saying very little else. Called in to get a hit, take out the competition by the looks of it.'

'I need to get in touch with Justin. The diamond came through a fence in Aberdeen, but he's not telling me who it is. I'm going upstairs to talk to Susannah. She's a possibility for a name. Otherwise, Justin's going to have a lot of footwork to do.'

Kirsten left Dominic and Carrie-Anne with their prisoners and made her way up several decks into a crew cabin. Normally, there would be two people in the room but the captain had cleared it. Susannah Small was sitting tied to a chair and Kirsten recognised the captain's first mate sitting in the room with her. She gave the man a nod, then asked him politely to leave the room.

'How long are you going to be? It looks bad just hanging out around outside the cabin,' said the first mate. 'You don't do anything down here as a first mate.'

Kirsten understood what he meant and told him to come back in ten minutes. With that, she turned to look at Susannah Small.

Hutchinson was right. She sure was attractive and Kirsten could see why the man was smitten with her, but she also saw a very frightened woman.

'Susannah, I think you're caught up in a bloody mess. I'm not sure you're aware, but Hutchinson's quite a bad man. He does a lot of things on the dark side of life, somewhat of a gang lord. He's into drugs, everything else. Now I know you're not. I know you're just somebody who's met him. You're his bit on the side. Something nice when the wife won't do.'

She saw Susannah flinch and genuinely felt sorry for the woman. 'He didn't tell you? Oh yes, he's married, kids, but that's not the worst of it. He is a very nasty piece of work, and what he's done with you, he's helped you to be part of his organisation; he's had you searching for something on this ship, a diamond. He's had you going through passenger lists. Something you probably thought, Yes, it's not exactly kosher, but he's only looking for something small. Did he tell you it could end like this? Did he tell you about the fact he holds a gun and he would kill people?'

The girl was shaking.

'But it's okay. You're not involved. What I do need is everything he told you lately because you see, I've got a situation here where this vessel is in jeopardy, all your crewmates, and I'm sure you've got friends amongst them, could end up down in the drink. I need you to start telling me everything Hutchinson told you.'

It was like a volcano had erupted. The girl just couldn't stop talking. It took Kirsten a moment to weed out all of the unnecessary rubbish that was in there. Susannah was starting to cry, panicked about what she'd seen and what she'd got into, and part of Kirsten felt like she should lean forward, hold her tight and tell her it was going to be all right because they weren't interested in her; she was just a pawn who was used. Then she told Kirsten about how Hutchinson's grandma's diamond had been taken and was now on board the vessel because he'd traced it through Aberdeen, through a man there.

Kirsten leaned in. 'Did he tell you the name?'

'He didn't tell me who the man was, no.'

'Did he tell you anything else around that? What had he done just before it?'

'He picked me up something in a jeweller's. This.' The girl pulled out a necklace with a heart hanging on the end and made of gold. Kirsten watched her rip it off her neck. 'Is this how easy I am?' she said.

'You weren't to know,' said Kirsten. 'You weren't to know. Which jeweller's?'

'It's on an alleyway. The centre of Aberdeen. Burns Way, they call it. Burns Way. Some modern little precinct.'

'That's where he bought you that, and then he talked to his fence. How soon after, do you know?'

'He went straight there. He said it was around the corner.' Kirsten tried not to leap in the air and squeal with delight. It was the break she needed. There was a knock at the door, and she opened it to see the first mate. The man came inside, standing almost to attention beside Kirsten.

'It's okay,' she said to Susannah, 'you've helped me greatly. You're probably going to lose your job because you did do things that you shouldn't have done for this man, but we won't be after you. In fact, you may have helped save us all.' She turned to the first mate. 'She doesn't leave this cabin but treat her well. Make sure she gets fed, but she has no outside contact until the matter's resolved that we have in hand.'

The first mate nodded. Kirsten made her way outside and up to her own cabin. Once inside, she contacted Justin Chivers.

'I wondered when you were going to come in. It's dead this side,' said Justin, 'I'm not going to get any more leads for you. Nobody seems to know nothing.'

'Burns Way in Aberdeen. There's a jeweller's there,' said Kirsten, 'and around the corner, operates the fence that took the diamond and put it on this ship. Find him. Find out how he did it, what he's got, and get back to me. We're under thirty hours here, Justin. Don't hang about.'

Chapter 20

Justin Chivers put the phone down, stood up from his chair and walked over to his coat hanging at his coat stand in the office. He checked he had his car keys, put the coat on, and grabbed his umbrella. He was wearing a pair of slacks, a shirt, and a tie and considered what else he needed with him. Quickly, he packed away his laptop and two minutes later was downstairs walking out the front door towards his car parked several streets away.

The time was almost midnight, and he was on his way to Aberdeen. The roads were clear on his way out of Inverness, and he drove steadily, only stopping once to pick up a cup of tea at a late-night garage. He passed through Nairn and then bypassed Elgin, out towards the city where his boss had been only twenty-four hours ago. As he drove, he looked up Burns Way on his map on the computer and discovered it was right in the centre of Aberdeen. There was a new shopping arcade, a mix of the old and the young, by the looks of it, slapped in like they did so often these days amongst some grander buildings. Grander in the sense of having stunning fixtures high up that people never looked at, but also significant dilapidation that came with age.

Justin thought this was a lesson for life. Older people always did seem grander, had the classier touches. It's just that the body didn't always work. He wasn't sure he wanted to get old, but on the other hand, maybe it was better than doing this.

At half past two, Justin had parked up and made his way towards the shopping arcade. Burns Way was locked off, but taking a set of lock-pick keys, Justin was able to enter, taking less than thirty seconds to open the lock that had sealed the gate across the entrance to the shopping arcade. Once inside, he located the jewellers and stood looking around him, wondering where Hutchison would've gone.

Around the corner, he thought. *Around the corner.* He made his way off to his right, went around the corner, and found the gents' lavatories. *Possibly not*, thought Justin. This time he went back and took the left turn, and found it ended in a small alcove with a door. Picking the door open, he stepped out into a back alley and strode five hundred yards off to his right. He could see no shop that would indicate there was a fence living within it.

Justin made his way back and walked the other direction until he saw what was effectively a high-class pawn shop. In the window was jewellery, locked up with cross hatch grills in front of it, but still on display. Justin looked up above the shop and saw a flat of some sort, windows that said there were occupiers above.

He took his umbrella and rapped the door with the handle. There was nothing except the bark of a dog in the distance. Even the city was quiet now. He could hear the occasional car going up and down a road somewhere, but there was little else. He rapped the door again, this time harder. As he looked up, he saw a curtain move in the window above. Maybe someone was looking down, but he couldn't be sure, because there was no light on. He rapped a third time, this time loud enough to wake the hounds of hell.

Justin smiled when he saw a light at the back of the shop come on. The door opened slightly, and he saw a woman in a dressing gown looking at him. He swore she could only be about nineteen.

'What's up? How can I help you?' asked the girl.

'I need to speak to the proprietor,' said Justin.

'That's me,' said the girl.

'No,' said Justin, 'the real proprietor. It's quite urgent. Mr. Hutchinson sent me.'

The girl's face fell, but then she recovered herself and opened the door, putting her hand out. 'Please come in,' she said and closed the door behind Justin. She went to the far side of the room and flicked on the lights. Justin also noticed that she had loosened her dressing gown somewhat, making sure that he had a chance to observe her more thoroughly. A bit of a waste, he thought to himself, but with practiced ease, he apparently became engrossed in her. 'I'll just get Mr. Goodway,' she said.

'Your father?' asked Justin. The girl shook her head.

'I hope I didn't disturb you two.' The girl turned and grinned, clearly playing the enticing woman, and again, Justin smiled back as if she was holding his attention. She disappeared out the rear of the shop and Justin began to look around it. With the lights now on, he saw a cavern of knick-knacks, trivia, but as he got closer to some of them, he saw their true worth. Many people in here would think this was a load of junk. Not Justin, for he did have a classical upbringing and he could recognise reasonable antiques when he saw them. He gently picked up a vase and looked at the mark underneath. Surprising, he thought, but certainly worth the £250 the man was looking for it.

'Do you mind putting that down? It's rather expensive,' said a voice behind him.

'Ah, Mr. Goodway. Nice of you to accommodate me at this time of night.' The girl appeared again, still in her dressing gown, half hanging open, and made her way over to Justin. She took his arm, clinging to it, looked up into his face and asked if she could get him anything.

'Do you do a decent whisky?' he said.

'Something hot and spicy for you, would that not be more appropriate?' said the girl. Inside, Justin nearly burst out laughing. Maybe she hadn't much experience in this, and he reckoned she was the man's daughter.

'Maybe not,' said Justin. 'I think I'm okay.'

'What is it you're wanting?' asked the man.

'I'm just looking for something for Mr. Hutchinson,' said Justin. 'Some diamonds, perhaps. Do you hold many?'

'We have a selection. Although I don't see the need for disturbing a man at this time of night.'

'He's in quite a rush for them. I'm sure you'd accommodate him.' Justin saw the man move towards a cabinet and then bend down behind it. Justin tensed slightly but tried to control himself for the girl was still on his arm.

Mr. Goodway brought up a tray and pulling back the cover of it, Justin saw the gleam of diamonds underneath. They sparkled as the lights bounced off them and Justin made his way over, the girl still tagging onto his arm.

'Would you mind if I pick them up and have a look?' said Justin. 'You wouldn't have an eyeglass handy?'

The man bent down again, put an eyeglass in front of Justin, and watched as Justin picked up one of the diamonds, looking at it. He had absolutely no idea about this. Diamonds were not his thing, but he hoped that his face was mulling over enough to give the idea of someone with a bit of taste.

'Rather good,' he said. 'We're looking at possibly ten of them, if that's all right.'

He felt the girl grab his arm tighter. 'Maybe you could stay for a while. It's late; you could take them in the morning,' she said.

The hairs on Justin's neck pricked up and he glanced out of the corner of his eye to see Mr. Goodway bending slightly. Justin's left hand reached out. He grabbed his umbrella that had been sitting up against the cabinet that Mr. Goodway was behind. Justin kept his face pointed at the girl, but the corner of his eye watched Mr. Goodway's shoulders start to rise. As they did so, he shoved the girl away hard.

The man rose and Justin could see the arms were tighter together. Without hesitation, he took the umbrella, smacked the man in the face once, then twice, before skipping around the back of the cabinet and kicking hard into the back of the man's legs. He hooked his neck with the umbrella while the man was still stunned, and pulled him down to the floor. He saw the weapon in the man's hands and reached down, twisting the man's wrist until it fell. Justin then kicked it far away. He put his foot on the man's chest, telling him not to move and took the umbrella, pressing it into the man's stomach.

'That's not really the service I was looking for,' he said.

The girl came forward. 'Don't hurt him,' she said. 'Don't hurt him.'

'Just get out of here,' said Mr. Goodway. 'You don't need to see this.' The girl went to turn, but Justin reached over with the umbrella, hooking her shoulder with the handle.

'No, you don't,' he said. 'You're staying here. Think I want you disappearing to the next room for a gun? On your knees now.' She knelt down, but even now she was trying to entice him.

'Take off the belt of the dressing gown, please,' said Justin. He kept a foot hard on the chest of Mr. Goodway, pressing it just enough so the man was struggling to breathe. 'Now wrap the belt under your wrists,' said Justin. Once the girl had done so, he tightened it. 'Now face down on the floor,' he said to her, but instead, she leaned forward in front of him.

'Would you rather me stay like this?' she said.

'I'm afraid that sort of thing doesn't work for me, love,' and with that, he reached out, grabbed her hair, and forced her to the floor.

'Right, then. Mr. Hutchinson said you didn't tell him what happened with the diamonds he was looking for. He said even when he threatened your family, you wouldn't speak. So, he said I should come along and extract the information from you. I need you to talk,' said Justin, pressing down hard on the man's chest. He also reached over with his umbrella, flicking a button on it and revealing a blade at the bottom. 'Because if you don't, I may have to get rather unpleasant with your daughter here.'

'Please don't,' wheezed the man.

'Mr. Hutchinson doesn't pay me to accept pleas of forgiveness or demands on my supposed kindness. I guess I am kind at times. My nephews tell me I am,' said Justin, 'but unfortunately, they're not here. So, it won't bother me at all if I have to take the *appropriate* action, shall we say?'

Justin gave a piercing glare at the man as he shook but the

man's eyes kept darting up high in the room. Justin looked up and saw a row of urns, ornate and fashionable.

'You put them in there,' he said suddenly. The man's face gave away the truth of what Justin had just said. 'Blimey,' said Justin. 'That's clever. An urn. An urn for who?' The man refused to speak, despite Justin pressing harder and harder.

'You'll have a sales book here, won't you?' said Justin. 'Let's hope there's a name in it,' he said, and tapped the girl on the back of the head with the umbrella, the blade having closed inside it again. 'If you'd be so kind, my dear, as to go and get the sales book and place it on the cabinet in front of me. Once you've done that you can resume your prone position.'

The girl stood up, walked over, and came back with a ledger, all the time trying to entice Justin again. In some ways, he thought she was better at handling the situation than her father. The ledger that she left on the cabinet in front of him was leather bound and he flicked through it, seeing that there were indeed sales records.

'So nice when people don't use the computer these days. These old-style methods are much better, don't you think?' he said to the man on the floor. He simply wheezed back.

Flicking to the rear of the book, Justin found sales from the previous week. He read quickly, although the man's handwriting was difficult. 'Ah,' he said. 'It says here an urn, an urn for Mrs. MacIver. Oh, hang on, some special instructions with it. Sent to *Her Majesty's Pride*. Marvellous. Well,' said Justin, 'thank you for being so helpful. Although I'd be remiss if I didn't say this: a father like you shouldn't let his daughter run around like that trying to entice grown men. Please, neither of you get up. I will look inside the shop window. If you've risen within the next five minutes, I shall come back in because I know I can't trust you to keep your mouths shut. I'll therefore make sure it stays shut permanently. Good day to you, sir,' said Justin, flicking the ledger closed with the handle of his umbrella. As he entered the street, he turned back and looked in the window, but he could see the girl face down, not moving.

From the position he was in, he could only see the legs of the father, still lying, feet pointed up to the ceiling. *Cooperation is so good*, thought Justin. He picked up his phone as he walked away. *Now the boss will be pleased. She was probably worried about leaving me here on my own. Still, sometimes I feel like people don't know me at all.*

Chapter 21

It was three in the morning, but Kirsten was waiting up, aware that Justin would be in Aberdeen by now. In some way, she was cursing herself having brought her three field operatives on board the vessel and leaving only Justin behind. Like everyone within the service, he was trained to some degree in fieldwork, but it was at such a low level by comparison to the likes of Dominic or even Kirsten.

She'd advised her colleagues to get an hour's sleep. After all, they'd been through the mill that night already. She'd taken a visit from the captain who was gradually becoming more and more desperate about the situation his vessel was in. One thing that bothered Kirsten was there were too many parties involved, too easy for things to go wrong. Furrer had people on board and some of them had been dispatched, but there could be others, and how many other interested parties as well? Hutchinson had been rather naïve, thinking he could come on and then simply buy the diamond off whoever was carrying it.

He'd been wrong in that but maybe he was being truthful when he said it was really a chance to get away and see Susannah again. For all the butchery of the man, he seemed to be very fond of her, not that that would do him any good. He'd lied to her about who he was, and she'd seen the real face of the world he lived in. At least that was one win so far, but it would be nothing unless she could secure the safety of this vessel.

Kirsten's mobile went. She jumped from the bed, grabbing it.

'What have you got, Justin?'

'Yes, nice to hear from you as well,' he said. 'Yes, I'm fine. I've come through unscathed.'

'You're phoning me, so you must have done. Now, what's up?'

'I paid a visit to your fence in the middle of the night. A rather nice young woman tried to entice me, but I fought her away and managed to secure the method of delivery of the diamonds onto the vessel.'

'Which was?' said Kirsten.

'They were sent to a Mrs MacIver.' Kirsten's heart jumped. MacIver. They'd been watching the MacIvers. They knew they were involved. Well, one of them was. 'There's an urn been sent to a Mrs. MacIver,' said Justin. 'I believe the diamond is inside of it.'

'So, it wasn't carried, taken away?'

'No. The man's ledger said it was sent. So, I assume it's been handled by the ship's staff and placed into the care of Mrs. MacIver, no doubt.'

'Good work, Justin. Get yourself back to base. We might still have need of you.'

'Oh, how kind of you. I thought I might catch an hour's sleep.'

'Look,' said Kirsten. 'I've got less than twenty-four hours.

We need to get onto this and quick.'

'What would you have me do?' asked Justin.

'Get in touch with Anna. Tell her what's happening. See if she can find any help from London.'

'I doubt it. I think if they had anything they'd have told you by now. The situation's getting critical,' said Justin.

There it was. Such a simple statement but coming from someone who obviously had experience. He was talking about how London worked. Why would you unless you knew how London worked? Kirsten wondered how far the cover of Justin Chivers went. How close was he really to Anna?

'You're right,' said Kirsten. 'I've got work to do here. Get yourself back. Be on the end of the phone. I might need you though I'm not sure why. Well done.'

'Wow, thank you. I'd ask you for dinner,' he says, 'but I think we both know that's not really appropriate anymore.' Kirsten smiled, realised the man couldn't see it, and so just gave a simple 'No.' Closing the call, she made her way up from her cabin to the cabin of Dominic and Carrie-Anne. Banging on the door, she stepped inside when Dom opened it, and saw Carrie-Anne coming down the stairs.

'Okay, Justin managed to find out that the urn's come on board addressed to Mrs. MacIver.'

Dom's eyes widened. 'We're tailing them.'

'Yes, you said there were three on board previously. We need to get hold of the three of them. See who's got an urn.' Dominic pulled out a piece of paper and started writing down cabin numbers. 'Okay,' said Kirsten, 'I'm going to go and interview them all. I'll pay a visit to the one two decks down. The one that's three decks down, Dom, you keep an eye on. I'll get to her straight after. Carrie-Anne, if you can find the one in the budget accommodation, that would be great.'

'Where's the vessel now?' asked Dominic.

'We're leaving Shetland making our way towards Stornoway,' said Kirsten. 'We haven't got long to tidy this up.' Kirsten made her way down two decks and knocked on the cabin door of the first Mrs. MacIver. It took three blows on the door before a woman opened it, wrapped up in an old-fashioned nightgown.

'Sorry to bother you, ma'am,' said Kirsten, 'ship security.'

The woman looked at her. 'Ship security? Why do you want me?'

She's not even asked for ID or anything, thought Kirsten. Kirsten was still dressed in T-shirts and jeans. She marvelled at how people would believe anything. 'I'm sorry,' said Kirsten, 'Can I come in?'

'If you're security, of course,' said the woman and led Kirsten into the moderately sized cabin. There was a bed in the far corner, a balcony, smaller than Dom and Carrie-Anne's, and a very small living area in which the woman invited Kirsten to sit down.

'Can I just check?' Kirsten asked. 'Your name is Mrs. MacIver.'

'It's Juliet MacIver, yes,' said the woman. Kirsten noted she was in a room with a double bed. 'May I ask if you have an urn with you at this time?'

The woman burst into tears. Kirsten watched her face closely. The tears seemed to be genuine.

'Yes, I have an urn,' she said. 'Well, not here. It's being held for me by the ship's staff. You see, John died recently. We were planning to come on here for our golden wedding anniversary, but John passed away. I didn't have time to pick up his ashes. They weren't ready before I came here. I decided to come anyway. You don't often get a chance like this paid for by my daughter. I thought it would be a time for a bit of reflection to talk about him to myself. I don't know if you've ever been bereaved, but sometimes you want space on your own. Sometimes you don't want everybody with you. Feels like he's here with me.'

The woman sniffed before continuing. 'I'm taking him to Stornoway, up to Ness where we lived for a large part of our life. It was his express wish to be reunited with the sea, and for me to send him home to it.'

Kirsten felt like a ghoul intruding on the woman's privacy, but she was convinced she was genuine. Stepping outside of the cabin for a moment, she called Justin asking him to check the woman's records. He did so and found that her husband had indeed died. Kirsten then made her way to the crew that looked after the baggage that was stowed long-term. She saw the clerk in his office, and he led her to the urn that had come on board.

'I actually handled that one myself,' he said. 'The driver from the delivery company passed that to me. It matched up with what the woman had said. She even had a delivery note indicating where the urn would be delivered.'

'That came in to you, and you've put it there, and you haven't done anything with it since?' said Kirsten.

'That's correct, ma'am.'

'Can you do me a favour?' asked Kirsten. 'Can you put it in the safe?'

The man looked at her quite quizzically. 'Just for me,' said Kirsten. 'Check with the captain if you need authorisation. It's not a problem taking it out when this journey is over and giving it to Mrs. MacIver. Where was she due to get off?'

'I believe it's at Stornoway, ma'am. Just let me check.' The man went through onto his computer records, 'Yes, she's off at Stornoway.'

Satisfied that the urn Mrs. MacIver had received was a genuine urn, received direct from the crematorium, Kirsten made her way to the second Mrs. MacIver. She passed Dominic in the corridor, not even giving him the time of day. She then rapped on the door. It was now closer to five in the morning and Kirsten heard movement inside. The door opened, and a Latino gentleman met her at the door.

'I'm sorry to bother you. I'm just looking for Mrs. MacIver.' Kirsten's arm was grabbed, and she found a gun being pointed at her belly.

'In,' said the man. Kirsten didn't react, simply walked forward, and let the man put a gun in her back, parading her into the middle of the room. On the floor was a woman in tears. She was middle-aged, her black hair falling to one side as she lay on the floor. She had a T-shirt on and trousers and had clearly been weeping for some time because the carpet of the cabin was wet.

'Who are you?' The man asked Kirsten.

'Ship security,' said Kirsten, hopefully.

'No, I have seen you about. Furrer said there would be others. Who are you?'

'Hutchinson sent me,' said Kirsten. 'He wants to do a deal. He wants the diamond. Do you have it?'

'Shut up,' said the man. 'On the floor.' Kirsten went down on her knees then had her hands tied up behind her. The man stood in front of her while the woman cried on the floor.

'What does Hutchinson know? We have not found the diamond, so what does Hutchinson know?'

'I went to a Mrs. MacIver above, and she has no urn. This woman here,' Kirsten lied, 'I had to keep her quiet, but she told me nothing as well.'

'I need to get this for Farrow. I owe Farrow. You tell me what you know, or I will beat it out of you.'

'No,' said Kirsten, 'Hutchinson doesn't play like that; you betray him, he'll kill me.'

The man slapped Kirsten hard across the cheek. The woman on the ground cried, begged the man to stop, but he raised his hand towards her, and she cried again.

'I said speak. Tell me what you know.' The man slapped Kirsten with the back of his hand again before he grabbed her hair and pulled it back. 'I told you to speak.'

'I told you, Hutchinson, he doesn't take kindly to that.' She spat into the man's face, but once again, he gave her the back of his hand, but this time, there was more venom in it. Kirsten had taken worse in the mixed martial arts ring. She knew how to handle a beating and she knew Dominic was outside. Surely the man would have got the point by now. He'd have gone past the door. He'd have heard surely.

'Maybe you need a different sort of encouragement,' the man said, and this time he turned around and lashed a kick at Kirsten's head. She saw it coming, timed her fall so that she was going with the kick, but she made it look impressive. She then sprawled on the ground, her hands behind her back. The man grabbed her arm pulling her up to her knees again.

'You want more of that?' he said. 'Or do I get a chain and beat you. Tell me what you know.'

Kirsten saw movement on the balcony and started to cry. 'Okay,' she said, 'okay.' She started to talk in a faint whisper.

The man grabbed her hair. 'I can't hear you; speak up.' He

pulled her close to him. 'I told you to speak.'

Kirsten went into a hoarse voice, pretending she was struggling with her tears. 'Hutchinson said—he said—'

There was a draught that suddenly went past Kirsten's face. The man must have felt it as well, for his head turned quickly. Kirsten heard the pounding fist that struck the man on the jaw. More punches followed. Kirsten saw Dominic press his knee in the man's back, pulling his hands together and holding his arms tight up the man's back.

'What took you so long?' said Kirsten.

'I thought my boss could handle herself. I don't want to rush in too quick with backup. You might get a little bit annoyed at me,' said Dominic.

With one hand, he held the man's arms up behind his back, although the man was unconscious anyway. Kirsten turned around and Dominic worked on the bonds until they came loose and they then together tied the man up.

'Take care of the girl,' said Kirsten to Dominic. 'The old lady up above is genuine. This one here doesn't have anything. It's time to go visit Carrie-Anne.'

Chapter 22

Kirsten made her way up to the deck, three down from the top level. Carrie-Anne met her, but this time wasn't dressed in heels and a sparkly dress. Instead, she had changed into a pair of slacks with a light blue top on but was looking as effervescent as ever. Kirsten thought compared to Carrie-Anne she must have looked a mess, because with some people, long nights didn't seem to affect them. With Kirsten, she looked as bedraggled as anyone.

'Where is she?' asked Kirsten.

'She's just having breakfast with a number of people. I'm not sure she knows them though,' said Carrie-Anne. 'More like she found them and got to sit in amongst them. She seems fairly jovial, but I've been keeping an eye on her, so I haven't been inside her cabin. Maybe that's her plan.'

'Yes, I think I'll turn it over. How long has she been there?'

'Forty minutes,' said Carrie-Anne, 'so she could be leaving soon.'

'Do you think she'll go back to a cabin?' asked Kirsten.

'No idea. I haven't observed her for long enough. Probably best to wait and see.'

Given the likelihood that this could be the woman they were

looking for, Kirsten decided against confronting her straight away. If something went wrong with the diamond, the vessel could be in danger. Instead, she let the woman finish her breakfast, and together with Carrie-Anne, she tailed her back to her own cabin. Once she was there, Kirsten rapped the door.

'Just a moment,' said the woman. Then she opened the cabin door looking rather perplexed.

'Sorry to bother you. Ship security. We've just had some reports about possible intruders in the people's rooms. I just wanted to make sure you were okay.'

'I'm fine, I've just been for breakfast,' said the woman.

'Your name, sorry,' asked Kirsten.

'Anne MacIver,' said the woman.

'Sorry to bother you, Mrs. MacIver, but if I could just take a quick look around. Wouldn't want anybody to be hiding in here.'

'Well, there's not a lot of room to hide in, in fairness,' said the woman. Kirsten made her way in and found out that the woman was telling the truth. It was slightly bigger than Kirsten's room, but not by much. Looking inside, Kirsten could see everything was neatly packed away. There was no visible urn.

'Are you on your own?' asked Kirsten.

'Yes,' the woman said. 'Unfortunately, my husband wasn't able to come with me.'

'I'm sorry to hear that. What was the reason?'

'He got called away suddenly.'

Kirsten felt like pushing it because everything that woman was saying could be taken different ways. Was she playing her, trying to find out if Kirsten knew about the urn?

'Well, there's clearly no one here,' said Kirsten, deciding not to hedge her bets. 'But if you do see anyone, please feel free to contact us. We'll be in there straight away.'

Kirsten left the cabin. Half an hour later, Carrie-Anne called in over the radio that Mrs. MacIver was leaving her cabin and she appeared to have her swimsuit with her. While Carrie-Anne followed her up to the swimming pool, Kirsten returned to the cabin. With ease, she managed to open the cabin door using a passkey given to her by the captain. She then began tearing through the room, opening every cupboard. Every nook and cranny was searched, but there was no urn. She went out on the balcony and checked, but again, there was nothing.

Everything seemed normal. Just clothes, lots of clothes. A few jigsaws, books to read, games to play. Even the ID of the woman said Mrs. MacIver on it. Whoever she was, she was good. After an hour of searching, Kirsten decided there was nothing to find. Making sure the room was the way she had found it, Kirsten exited.

'Is she still in the pool?' asked Kirsten.

'Charlie here. Affirmative, still swimming up and down.'

'How far away from Stornoway, are we?' asked Kirsten.

'Delta here. I'd say we've got maybe an hour, two at the most.'

'Time to make our move then,' said Kirsten. 'It's not in the cabin. We need to find out where she's hidden it.'

'Wait,' said Carrie-Anne, 'she's getting out of the pool.'

'We'll take her right now. Let her get changed. Make sure she's got her stuff with her, then we'll intercept her.'

'Roger, wilco.'

Kirsten made her way up through the decks until she got to the swimming pool area. She saw Carrie-Anne on the far side, and then saw Mrs. MacIver making her way out of the changing rooms. With a grin on her face, the woman was jovial, talking to different people, although Kirsten wasn't sure she knew them. She entered one of the lifts, Kirsten watching it closely. Carrie-Anne made for the lift beside it.

Kirsten watched Anne MacIver's lift go down, and then advised to Carrie-Anne that the woman was four floors down. Carrie-Anne was already inside her own lift, and it took her some twenty seconds before she descended.

'I'm about to get into the lift,' said Kirsten. 'Have you got eyes on?'

'Charlie here, negative. Stand by.' Kirsten felt her heartbeat rise slightly, but she was sure Carrie-Anne would clock her again in a second.

'Charlie here, no sign of target.'

'Delta,' said Kirsten, 'are you on the floor too?'

'Delta here, no sighting.' Kirsten looked at the lift in front of her. It had just gone up past the swimming pool level, continuing to the very top deck.

'The elevator's now gone right to the top. I'm in pursuit. Keep on that floor in case she's passed you.'

Kirsten ran as hard as she could up a set of stairs that led to the outside. Although the swimming pool was at the top of the vessel, there were another two levels above it which consisted of promenade rings around the swimming pool. They were significantly higher up but Kirsten was able to take stairs to gain access to them.

Once up there, she looked along the promenade deck and spied Mrs. MacIver dressed in her coat, bag over her shoulder. As Kirsten watched, an Arab man was coming from the other direction to the woman. Kirsten began to run towards them.

Mrs. MacIver didn't seem to flinch as the Arab man made his way closer, giving Kirsten the idea that they were in league together. But then she watched him suddenly snatch the bag off the woman's shoulder. The woman shouted at him and he began to run. Kirsten ran at him, taking him on in a head-on encounter. As he tried to sidestep, she went down low, flung her arms around him, her shoulder driving into his midriff as her arms wrapped him up. He smacked down on his backside.

As Kirsten recovered, she grabbed the bag off him, and tipping it up, she watched the contents fall onto the deck. The man tried to reach past Kirsten, but she elbowed him in the face before turning around and smacking him hard again. As she turned back, she saw the contents of the bag on the floor of the deck. There was a towel and a swimsuit with a bathing cap.

She ruffled through the items, but there was nothing else there and she turned and looked up to see Mrs. MacIver standing at the edge of the vessel, looking out. She gave a wave before opening her coat. Kirsten got up on her feet and ran towards the woman.

From inside her coat, the woman produced a small urn, extremely similar to the one Kirsten had seen in the depths of the boat that was owned by the grieving Mrs. MacIver. The woman was only a short distance away and clearly, she was looking where to throw the urn, so much so that Kirsten was able to make up the ground. As Anne MacIver went to throw the urn overboard, Kirsten put her hand up and blocked it, and the urn fell onto the deck.

Kirsten turned to grab the urn, but she then felt her neck being pulled at. The woman had some strength in her, but Kirsten was surprised by a knife suddenly driving into her arm. She collapsed onto the floor. The woman stepped over her and drove a foot onto Kirsten's head. Kirsten watched her pick up the urn again, but reaching out with her good arm, Kirsten grabbed her ankle, throwing it upwards, tripping the woman onto the deck again.

'You bitch,' Anne MacIver shouted at her. Kirsten received another kick to the head, but she shrugged it off, thankful for the years of training in the ring, forcing her to first protect herself, and then to find a way out.

But the woman wasn't concerned with Kirsten. Instead, she reached and grabbed the urn before stumbling over to the side. Once again, she went to throw it out to the sea, but Kirsten had leapt to her feet and jumped on the woman's back. She managed to place a hand on the urn. They fought this way and that with a couple of surprised bystanders looking at them.

Kirsten was in pain, her arm hurting from the knife wound, but she fought through that, struggling to maintain a grip on the urn. Suddenly, Mrs. MacIver back-butted her, and Kirsten felt the blow on the fore of her head. It was hard, and Kirsten's hand slipped, but one remaining hand caught the top of the urn. She hung on to it and as she tumbled to the ground, the lid came away in Kirsten's hand. The rest of the urn began to tip.

Kirsten lay on the deck looking through the see-through panelling that protected passengers from falling off the ship. She saw the ashes inside take to the wind, and then the urn fell down to the sea.

'You stupid bitch,' the woman said looking at Kirsten. 'It's gone. It's gone. It's worth millions. That was worth millions to me.' The woman dove for Kirsten, hands locking out straight to Kirsten's throat. The knife wound was causing Kirsten's arm to begin to seize and she fought with her other arm to throw a punch at the woman.

Then from behind her, someone dragged the woman off her. She saw the Arab man she had tackled looking at her.

'So, it's gone,' he said. 'You have put my country's heritage in the sea.' He took a radio from inside his jacket.

'Don't,' said Kirsten. 'It's not worth it. It's not worth it.'

'You've besmirched my country's name. We'll be a laughing-stock. It's only right that we take vengeance on you. We have our honour to think about.'

'But you're still on board,' said Kirsten.

'You know nothing of honour.'

The man said some words in a foreign language Kirsten didn't understand and then he grabbed Mrs. MacIver on the floor, picking her up.

'You who have lost this, you who have banished my country's emblem, you shall pay.' He picked her up and grabbed the woman, throwing her up and over the protective rail. One hand clung on, but the man came down on it hard with his fist, causing the woman's hand to open and she screamed as she fell down to the waves beneath.

Kirsten's eyes were wide, the horror of what the man had just done, but he stared back at her.

'Do you think I'm barbaric after what she did to my country? I only sent her on her way early, but soon we will all go. They have activated the bombs. It's time your country found out the dishonour they did to us.'

Chapter 23

Kirsten tapped her earpiece. 'Charlie, Delta, bombs on board, bombs have been activated. Delta, activate your search pattern worked out with the captain. All the areas you worked out. Begin the search now.'

Considering what she just said, Dom's reply of, 'Delta, Roger' seemed very inadequate. Kirsten picked herself up off the floor. The Arab gentleman had turned away and she went after him, grabbing his shoulder with her good arm and throwing him against the edge of the ship.

'Where?' she cried. 'Where are they?'

'On board,' he sneered, 'but don't worry. You have fifteen minutes. Fifteen minutes while we tell the world, fifteen minutes while we get cameras on you, fifteen minutes for your government to sweat.'

Kirsten drove a knee up into the man's groin and he buckled over. He tried to put his hands out to grab her, but she continued pounding him, striking again with her knee before taking him down to the floor. A member of the crew ran up towards her and she turned, shouting at him.

'Tell the captain, tell the captain, it's come to the worst. We have fifteen minutes to find them. He'll know what I mean.'

The man looked at her. 'Can you get off that gentleman, please?'

'No, I work for the government. We're in trouble. Get the message to the captain now.'

The man looked at her for a moment. Maybe he was just unsure that he wanted to take her on given she was holding an Arab gentleman down on the ground and beating him up with one arm. The crew member ran away, and Kirsten glanced at her arm and the knife wound on it. There was blood coming from it and she probably needed to wrap it up tight, but at the moment, she had more pressing concerns.

'Where?' she asked the man again, bouncing his head off the deck. 'Where?'

'All on board,' he said smiling. Then Kirsten saw his mouth begin to foam. His eyes rolled, his head went back, and the man lay there dead.

No, she thought but jumped to her feet and started staggering forward. She stopped momentarily and began to rip her t-shirt with one arm. Once she had pulled apart a large enough piece of it, she put it on her bad arm and tried to tie it up rather unsuccessfully. She turned to a man standing close by. He was agape at the entire situation.

'Tie this arm up tight.' He looked at her. 'Did you just see what I did to that guy? Would you tie my arm up tight?'

The man reacted quickly, tying it up and then running away from her. She also began to run, to take the stairs down to the lower decks. The ship's Tannoy began to sound the evacuate ship signal. Kirsten reckoned fifteen minutes would not be enough. People began milling around.

'Delta, come in. Status?'

'Delta here. I have the list and working through. Charlie's

with me. Continuing down the vessel.'

'Roger.' Kirsten made her way down, stair after stair beneath her. At times she felt slightly faint, but she kept going until she got to three decks from the bottom of the vessel and found Dom searching behind a bulkhead.

'One here,' he said, 'I've got one. I'm trying to disarm it now.'

'How many do we have?' asked Kirsten.

'How I should I know!' said Dom. 'We have no idea. Here's the list of positions that are significant.'

'Do you have anybody other than the three of us?' asked Kirsten.

'Got a couple of the crew on it as well, but the captain is tied up with evacuating the vessel.'

'How long have we got left? He said fifteen minutes up there.'

'It has taken you about four to get down at least,' said Dom. 'We've maybe ten minutes left.'

Kirsten tore the list towards the bottom. 'I'll cover these bits. You get on that bomb, get everyone else after the rest of them.' With that, Kirsten tore off to the other side of the vessel. She read Dom's instructions. Making her way through was chaotic as people were running here and there. Thankfully, most of the passengers were now being pulled into muster areas to start to board lifeboats, but down in the crew quarters, it was bedlam. Kirsten made her way round one corner and found an area that was seen as significant. She searched in, up and behind, but found nothing and made her way off to her next target.

'Charlie here, found one. Able to lift it, so taking it up top to dump it.'

'Kilo here, Roger. Delta, can you move yours?'

'Negative, but I'm disarming.'

Kirsten continued to run along the vessel. She checked three more areas, but when she got to her fourth, she saw a crewman looking at something. 'Is there . . . ?' she began and the man simply nodded at her. Kirsten looked and saw a bomb, a small square device over a clear activation pad and a numerical counter on it.

'Kilo. Found another one, I believe it may be mobile, taking it to the top.' Kirsten ran her arms around the device before confirming she could lift it off. It was magnetically attached, and she wasn't quite sure why blowing out this particular section would cause the most damage to the ship, but that wasn't her field. All she had to do was to get it up and overboard. Kirsten ripped the bomb off the wall much to the crewman's shock and then turned to him.

'Which way is quickest up to the top?'

'You could take the lift but with the alarm sounding, it might not work.'

'Which stairs then?' asked Kirsten, and the man pointed down the corridor. She made her way quickly, trying not to stumble, or worse still, fall over and drop the bomb, setting it off, but instead, ran measuredly. Arriving at the stairs she felt woozy, but she forced herself to breathe and take in air before she started climbing the stairs. Some people were coming down and she barked at them to get out of the way, driving herself up.

'I've got a bomb, get out of the way,' she yelled and watched as they turned and fled upwards. There were at least fifteen decks to climb. It took Kirsten a good five minutes to go up through all of them and by the time she reached the top, it said four minutes on the bomb. She made her way up to the promenade deck, ready to launch the bomb over the side, but when she looked down, she saw lifeboats at the edge.

She began to run round the promenade looking over the side, but there were lifeboats at either end, so she made for the stern of the vessel and looked out behind it. The vessel was coming to a stop, but a wake was still visible behind it. There was a life raft not far away but this would be the best bet because the other rafts were now freeing from the vessel all around. Looking at the counter, Kirsten saw two minutes and launched it over the side.

'Kilo has disposed of one in the rear. Charlie, status?'

'In your nine o'clock. Coming to your position.'

'Delta, status?'

'Delta has diffused. Looking for more.' Kirsten scanned the top deck. There was no one on the upper decks now. She urged Carrie-Anne over, but the woman needed no encouragement. As she reached Kirsten, she hurled her bomb over into the sea.

'I make it less than a minute,' said Kirsten.

'Agreed,' said Carrie-Anne, 'we may have to jump.'

'Not yet,' said Kirsten, 'we may not have got them all.' She went to hunker down behind a kiosk up on the promenade. It served drinks, moonlight cocktails, but inside was a large fridge, a heavy item and Kirsten put her back up against it. Carrie-Anne tucked in tight with her.

'Thirty seconds. Delta, status?'

'I haven't found any more. Have moved away to the middle of the ship in case any go off.'

'Roger.'

The next twenty seconds seemed like an age. Kirsten and Carrie-Anne held tight together, huddled up behind the large fridge, and waited. Kirsten's phone went off. It was Anna.

'They say they're going to do it now,' said Anna.

'I know,' said Kirsten, 'I know,' and then she heard the explosion. Kirsten felt the boat rock and a second explosion went off.

'Delta, status?'

'Middle of the ship. I can't feel anything. Heard that though. It's not from down here. It's not from down in the depths.'

With how loud the explosion had been, Kirsten reckoned it must have come from the top of the vessel. She went to open the door of the kiosk, but she couldn't move it. Together with Carrie-Anne, they kicked hard and the door eventually fell open. Kirsten looked out and realised that the promenade behind her was gone, having tumbled off into the sea.

'What's happening?' came the voice on the phone. 'What's going on?'

'Stand by,' said Kirsten. 'Delta, confirm again, no explosions down below.'

'On my way round now, I cannot find any.'

Kirsten leaned out of the door of the kiosk and had to swing around on it to make her way to a section of promenade that remained. Together with Carrie-Anne, they walked around the top of what still stood of the promenade. Looking down, they saw life rafts moving away from the ship. Together, they were able to climb down some steps, and route across where the swimming pool was, up to the other side of the promenade. Peering down on the other side, they saw more life rafts moving away.

'Anna, we've had explosions. It looks like we cleared the bombs from down below, the ones there to sink the vessel, but they put a couple up top. We've lost parts of the promenade, but I don't think anyone was up here except us.'

'We'll be sending people out to evacuate everyone. Stay safe.

See if you can identify anybody else on board, anyone still hostile.'

Kirsten slumped down and Carrie-Anne bent down to look at her arm. 'You need that seen to,' she said.

Kirsten smiled. 'Yes. Well at least we can get it seen to now. Anna wants us to check round for any more hostiles, but I think the big one's up. I guess they'll be sending in people a little more obvious than us to take care of things.

'Of course, they will,' said Carrie-Anne, and together they made their way down inside the vessel, waiting for the rescue parties to come on board. They sat down by the swimming pool, Kirsten lying down on a lounger, and Carrie-Anne sitting on a seat, amidst a dusty atmosphere. Dominic appeared from the deck below.

'I guess that's that,' said Dom. 'Where's the diamond though?'

'It looks like it went into the sea during my fight with Mrs MacIver. I managed to pull the lid off the urn. It tipped up and everything went down to the sea,' said Kirsten. 'Just that I never saw the diamond. It's meant to be a big one, isn't it? I thought the least I would have done is catch a glimpse of it. Then there was an Arab man who came along and tossed her in. Gave the order to set off the bombs.'

'All done and dusted though. London won't be happy,' said Dom. 'After all, we've been attacked.'

'We have,' said Kirsten, 'but it looks like the worst didn't happen from it. That was good prep, Dom. That was amazingly fine prep you did.'

Kirsten watched her team, tired but smiling, but something inside was kicking at her. She couldn't work out exactly what it was, but she would do. It would come to her, whatever was bugging her. She looked across at her arm where the blood was still seeping through.

'Dom, can you redo that arm for me? I really could do with a hand there.' He nodded and Kirsten laid back on the lounger. She would get the arm seen to, and then sort out what it was that was bugging her.

Chapter 24

Kirsten stood at the front of the Western Isles hospital in Stornoway. She'd been discharged some forty-eight hours after entering because they'd wanted to watch the wound that she had suffered. At first, it looked like it may become infected, but after two days, they declared that she was good to go, putting her arm in a sling and advised she could come out to the front door.

Kirsten stood there, looking at the windy day before her, but noting the bright blue sky. That was the thing about the Isle of Lewis, at least during her time here, back when she was a police officer. The days when it was sunny, the winds were wild, but when it was sunny, they were often the most spectacular of days. Having lay in her bed for the last two days being attended to, her mind had been churning over what had been bugging her, and it was as she came down in the lift about to be discharged that it struck her. She stood outside the hospital, picked up her mobile phone, and put a call in to Justin Chivers.

'It's Justin. How are you?'

'Good,' said Kirsten. 'The arm's going to be okay. A couple of weeks to get back to normal or something like that.'

'Well, Anna's happy with you guys. Well, happier than London.'

'I thought she'd be annoyed at us not having found the diamond.'

'Anna is a bit more realistic than others,' said Justin. 'There were no civilian casualties. Everyone that died was after the diamond. From the shootout at Strathpeffer all the way through to the boat, you didn't lose anybody that was innocent. She takes that as a win every time.'

'I guess the boat isn't going to be doing much for a while.'

'No, that's a bit of a slap in the face, and that's what London sees it as, but they'll rebuild the boat, and we'll start up again. You did good, boss,' said Justin.

'Well, I couldn't blow the first one in charge, could I? I take it the gang are back with you.'

'Yes. Dom and Carrie-Anne came in, but they took a day yesterday. When are you back over with us?'

'Probably tomorrow. I got something I want to do here first. Tell me, Justin, would you have the address of Mrs. MacIver?'

'Which one?' asked Justin.

'The old lady,' said Kirsten. 'You had three of them. One actually was a widow and had an urn coming to her.'

'Give me ten minutes.' With that Justin hung up. Kirsten was waiting for a taxi and had booked a place to stay in town, but she had a feeling she'd be going somewhere else first, so when the taxi arrived and Justin hadn't rung back, she asked him simply to wait, telling him to put it on the meter.

When Kirsten then received the call from Justin, she told the taxi driver to make his way over to Ness. The journey to the port of Ness took Kirsten over the Barvas moor. She marvelled at the sunlight stretching across the barren stretch of land. She saw the peat banks cut into the sides of banks and thought of her time here recently when she'd tried to protect a child who had been hunted down by gangsters.

When she arrived at the small cottage towards the top end of Ness, Kirsten made the taxi driver wait while she banged on the door. After several minutes, a neighbour poked her head out, coming over to speak to Kirsten.

'Sorry, I'm looking for Mrs. MacIver,' said Kirsten.

'Oh, she's not in. She's gone off up there to the harbour. Her husband used to go up there all the time in these last days when he was walking. Unfortunately, he died when he was away, so she wanted to bring him back to his place. I think she's gone off with his ashes.'

Kirsten's heart skipped a bit. 'Off to the harbour?'

'Yes,' said the woman, running a hand through her greying hair. 'I think you're meant to get permission and stuff, but I think she's just going to do it. To be honest, she's been through a lot recently, what with his illness and that, and then they had to fly away. They were booked to go on that boat and that as well. She's been just going through all that. But the guy came today from the delivery company. He said they had taken everything off and they sent up the urn by courier. She was quite worried about it.'

'In the harbour, right at the top?'

'Yes, yes,' she said, and Kirsten turned and bolted back to the taxi, leaving the woman quite aghast.

'Off to the harbour, quick,' said Kirsten. The bemused driver drove as quick as he could the short distance to the harbour. Kirsten ran along the large harbourside and saw at the end of it Mrs. MacIver, standing in a large coat, for it was as windy as it was bright and sunny. Temperatures in Ness never got particularly high but at this time of year, they certainly wouldn't be.

As Kirsten got close, she saw the woman lift the urn up in the air, take off the lid and then turn it upside down. Kirsten ran up beside her, throwing her arms into the swirling plume that was now drifting off towards the sea. The woman looked at her as the ashes continued to pour out.

'What are you doing?' she said. 'This is my husband. He's going out to the sea. He's going to the place he loved.'

'I know,' said Kirsten, 'and he is free to go.'

'What are you doing? Do you realise what I've been through? Do you realise what this means to me?'

'I do,' said Kirsten. 'But unfortunately, that's not your husband.'

'How do you mean?' the woman asked. 'Of course, it's him. They put him in the urn. They gave it to me from the ship.'

Kirsten felt a large weight in her hand. It had hit her hand just after the woman had tipped up the urn and started pouring the ashes out. She'd got there just in the nick of time. Kirsten opened her hand in front of the woman. There, amongst some grains of dust that had stuck to Kirsten's hand, was a diamond. It didn't look bright, covered in the ash, but Kirsten rubbed it and slowly its lustre was coming back.

'What's that?' asked the woman.

'That's what all the trouble was over,' said Kirsten. 'That's why there was a bomb on that boat. That's why I was trying to find out who you were.'

'How do you mean?' asked the woman.

'There was another Mrs. MacIver on board, and she was getting sent ashes as well. They both arrived, they were both signed in for, but unfortunately for some reason, the crewman who was looking after them managed to put yours under her name and gave it to her and hers to you. You never had yours, after they stored them safely below, but she took hers and she tried to throw it out off the boat because it was meant to go to somebody waiting below in a boat. I'm sorry, but your husband is scattered just off Stornoway, out there in the Minch.'

The woman turned and began to cry and Kirsten offered her shoulder, giving what comfort she could to the woman.

'I'm so sorry,' said Kirsten. 'You deserve none of this.' The weight of the woman's head on her shoulder was causing Kirsten's arm pain but she let the woman remain there until she'd gathered herself. Kirsten convinced her to go back in the taxi to her house. She remained there for an hour, making sure neighbours were available to help the woman after this new shock she'd had. Following that, she took a taxi back into Stornoway, checked into her accommodation before taking herself out for a stroll around the town she used to work in. She waited until nine o'clock that night before calling Anna Hunt.

'I'll be up immediately,' said Anna. 'We need to know about this. We need to keep it secure.'

'You need to tell no one, Anna; that's how we keep it secure. Send the plane up in the morning and I'll get on it. Nine o'clock, nothing too early, and we can go and meet Godfrey and return his precious diamond.'

'Good work,' said Anna. 'I really am quite impressed. If you'd only managed to stop the ship getting blown up, I could really have put you forward for some sort of award.'

Kirsten laughed on the phone at her. 'There is something you can do for me though,' she said. 'Tomorrow after I see

Godfrey, make sure I've got about a four or five-hour wait before I get the plane back up north.'

'Why?' asked Anna.

'I've got my own reasons.'

* * *

Kirsten shook Godfrey's hand, glad that the diamond was out of her care. Anna Hunt was there and was struggling not to smile as Godfrey had taken the diamond. Apparently, Kirsten had done a jolly good show, but in reality, Kirsten didn't care. Her work was done, and this was now playtime.

She sat on the park bench after seeing Godfrey and Anna disappear. Part of her was a little nervous. She was dressed in her jeans and T-shirt, for she'd come straight from Stornoway and hadn't had time to get dressed properly. Godfrey had looked at her rather bemusedly, but Anna had explained that she was on a tight schedule. Besides, the arrival of the diamond made Godfrey not care at all.

Kirsten was sitting looking at the park as a large limo pulled up in front of her. From one side of it, a man stepped out and came towards her. He stood before her, tipping a hat he had on and telling her that her car was ready. She looked up and saw a face she remembered from her last visit to London.

'I believe we've got some time to kill,' said Kirsten. 'Do you know any good coffee shops?'

'I believe so,' said the man, and he put his hand forward, allowing Kirsten to use it to get up. 'Sorry,' she said. 'I'm not dressed so neatly as before.'

'At least you're one of the real field types,' he said. 'I guess there might be something to talk over now when we have our coffee. I heard you did pretty well.'

'We did all right,' said Kirsten, 'but it's not what I want to talk about. I think it's time I found out a little bit more about you.'

Read on to discover the Patrick Smythe series!

Start your Patrick Smythe journey here!

Patrick Smythe is a former Northern Irish policeman who

after suffering an amputation after a bomb blast, takes to the sea between the west coast of Scotland and his homeland to ply his trade as a private investigator. Join Paddy as he tries to work to his own ethics while knowing how to bend the rules he once enforced. Working from his beloved motorboat 'Craigantlet', Paddy decides to rescue a drug mule in this short story from the pen of G R Jordan.

Join G R Jordan's monthly newsletter about forthcoming releases and special writings for his tribe of avid readers and then receive your free Patrick Smythe short story.

Go to https://bit.ly/PatrickSmythe for your Patrick Smythe journey to start!

About the Author

GR Jordan is a self-published author who finally decided at forty that in order to have an enjoyable lifestyle, his creative beast within would have to be unleashed. His books mirror that conflict in life where acts of decency contend with self-promotion, goodness stares in horror at evil, and kindness blindsides us when we at our worst. Corrupting our world with his parade of wondrous and horrific characters, he highlights everyday tensions with fresh eyes whilst taking his methodical, intelligent mainstays on a roller-coaster ride of dilemmas, all the while suffering the banter of their provocative sidekicks.

A graduate of Loughborough University where he masqueraded as a chemical engineer but ultimately played American football, Gary had worked at changing the shape of cereal flakes and pulled a pallet truck for a living. Watching vegetables freeze at -40'C was another career highlight and he was also one of the Scottish Highlands "blind" air traffic controllers.

These days he has graduated to answering a telephone to people in trouble before telephoning other people to sort it out.

Having flirted with most places in the UK, he is now based in the Isle of Lewis in Scotland where his free time is spent between raising a young family with his wife, writing, figuring out how to work a loom and caring for a small flock of chickens. Luckily, his writing is influenced by his varied work and life experience as the chickens have not been the poetical inspiration he had hoped for!

You can connect with me on:
- https://grjordan.com
- https://facebook.com/carpetlessleprechaun

Subscribe to my newsletter:
- https://bit.ly/PatrickSmythe

Also by G R Jordan

G R Jordan writes across multiple genres including crime, dark and action adventure fantasy, feel good fantasy, mystery thriller and horror fantasy. Below is a selection of his work. Whilst all books are available across online stores, signed copies are available at his personal shop.

The Nationalist Express (Kirsten Stewart Thrillers #4)
https://grjordan.com/product/the-nationalist-express
A country divided by a historic vote. The whisper of a bombing amongst the loyal few. Can Kirsten infiltrate an extreme nationalist agenda and prevent a disaster south of the border?

Scotland is once again in political turmoil as it returns to the debate of whether to remain part of the United Kingdom. Under all the paraphernalia of various vying parties, Kirsten and her team discover a scheme to promote the separation from the Union with a series of terrorist plots. And when London becomes the target, the stakes are raised significantly. Can the recently formed team remain impartial while bringing the nefarious scheme to light?

What does history matter when you can fix the future?

The Culling at Singing Sands (Highlands & Islands Detective Book 15)

https://grjordan.com/product/the-culling-at-singing-sands

A glamorous retirement village on an isolated island. A brutal killer culls the elderly starting with the oldest resident. Can Macleod discover the murderous motive and prevent the island graveyard from overflowing?

When the Isle of Eigg enjoys the opening of 'The Singing Sands' Later but Better Township', little do they realise that death is only round the corner for the new arrivals. Joy turns to sorrow as old friends meet a bloody end, and DI Macleod and DS McGrath are dispatched to investigate. As a determined clientele and some unseasonal weather hamper the investigation, the detectives must look to the past to prevent the dispatching of those seen to be past their time.

Even in paradise you're only one step from the grave!

Corpse Reviver (A Contessa Munroe Mystery #1)

https://grjordan.com/product/corspe-reviver

A widowed Contessa flees to the northern waters in search of adventure. An entrepreneur dies on an ice pack excursion. But when the victim starts moonlighting from his locked cabin, can the Contessa uncover the true mystery of his death?

Catriona Cullodena Munroe, widow of the late Count de Los Palermo, has fled the family home, avoiding the scramble for title and land. As she searches for the life she always wanted, the Contessa, in the company of the autistic and rejected Tiff, must solve the mystery of a man who just won't let his business go.

Corpse Reviver is the first murder mystery involving the formidable and sometimes downright rude lady of leisure and her straight talking niece. Bonded by blood, and thrown together by fate, join this pair of thrill seekers as they realise that flirting with danger brings a price to pay.

Highlands and Islands Detective Thriller Series

https://grjordan.com/product/waters-edge

Join stalwart DI Macleod and his burgeoning new DC McGrath as they look into the darker side of the stunningly scenic and wilder parts of the north of Scotland. From the Black Isle to Lewis, from Mull to Harris and across to the small Isles, the Uists and Barra, this mismatched pairing follow murders, thieves and vengeful victims in an effort to restore tranquillity to the remoter parts of the land.

Be part of this tale of a surprise partnership amidst the foulest deeds and darkest souls who stalk this peaceful and most beautiful of lands, and you'll never see the Highlands the same way again

The Disappearance of Russell Hadleigh (Patrick Smythe Book 1)

https://grjordan.com/product/the-disappearance-of-russell-hadleigh

A retired judge fails to meet his golf partner. His wife calls for help while running a fantasy play ring. When Russians start co-opting into a fairly-traded clothing brand, can Paddy untangle the strands before the bodies start littering the golf course?

In his first full novel, Patrick Smythe, the single-armed former policeman, must infiltrate the golfing social scene to discover the fate of his client's husband. Assisted by a young starlet of the greens, Paddy tries to understand just who bears a grudge and who likes to play in the rough, culminating in a high stakes showdown where lives are hanging by the reaction of a moment. If you love pacey action, suspicious motives and devious characters, then Paddy Smythe operates amongst your kind of people.

Love is a matter of taste but money always demands more of its suitor.

Surface Tensions (Island Adventures Book 1)
https://grjordan.com/product/surface-tensions
Mermaids sighted near a Scottish island. A town exploding in anger and distrust. And Donald's got to get the sexiest fish in town, back in the water.

"Surface Tensions" is the first story in a series of Island adventures from the pen of G R Jordan. If you love comic moments, cosy adventures and light fantasy action, then you'll love these tales with a twist. Get the book that amazon readers said, "perfectly captures life in the Scottish Hebrides" and that explores "human nature at its best and worst".

Something's stirring the water!